English for Food and Beverage Service

餐飲英文

鄭寶菁 編著

全華圖書股份有限公司

飲食是人們日常生活中不可或缺的;在「餐飲英文」一書中,不論是對於餐廳內的服務生、店經理、旅客、成功的商業人士,甚至是背包客,都將不斷致力提供有用的資訊。在「餐飲英文」中,我們可以化身為員工、顧客或是一位旅客,一再品嚐不同的美食。「餐飲英文」內的每一個單元都是有趣且貼近生活的資訊。「餐飲英文」內的每一個單元都是有趣且貼近生活的資訊。由訂位開始,至速食用餐、台灣珍珠奶茶、米其林指南《必比登夜市小吃》、以及多汁的牛排、令人垂涎欲滴的甜甜圈甜點及冰淇淋,本書將指引我們前往世界各地的美食之旅,讓讀者更渴望接觸世界及新知。

「餐飲英文」的編排符合世界各國美食的教學及實際應用,「餐飲英文」的架構幫助讀者更容易理解吸收,它提供了讀者沉浸式的學習法,彷彿置身在歐美國家中。每一個單元都精心挑選實際拍攝的圖片,包含令人垂涎的美食及飲品,以全彩的視覺饗宴帶給讀者更豐富的視覺享受。

「餐飲英文」提供餐飲行業更多更完善的資源及實際情境,讓教育工作者及學生能夠實際體驗歐美的餐飲文化,甚至餐飲服務的流程。我強烈推薦教師及學生閱讀此書,同時我亦推薦餐飲管理者及員工能夠藉由此書提昇自己的職涯水準。

「餐飲英文」能夠成為已在餐飲業工作者、甚至即將進入此領域的人一個良好的典範,更者幫助喜好於歐美旅行的旅客,「餐飲英文」將是一本最佳的隨身手冊。

總體來說,本書是一本適用於旅客、餐飲專業經理人及員工最佳的導覽手冊。

Lee yu ting

李玉鼎
金車集團 總經理

　　展閱鄭寶菁教授的餐飲英文後，誠摯推薦這本必讀的英文專書。在浩瀚的書海中，該類主題的書籍眾多，常讓我們不知如何選取，鄭教授的書籍在該類書籍中顯得格外的耀眼，因為這本書完全切合餐飲行業的英文，也是該專業領域中銷售最佳的書籍之一。

　　餐飲英文也許對於有些讀者來說認為很簡單，但實際上卻是相當難以精通的領域，尤其是對非以英文為母語的讀者。作者精心編排這本書將餐飲英文變得易於學習及吸收，藉著分割出不同情境的小單元，讓讀者一步一步藉著每一單元的學習逐步建立起餐飲英文的能力。單元內容有腦力激盪的設計，也有重要的會話表達和垂涎三尺的圖片，以突顯出每個單元應有的特色。不管是由觀光者的角度或導遊者的觀點，都可發現書中的會話展現了眾多餐飲文化的特質，使讀者完全了解實務上所面對的環境，且本書加入許多實際案例的演練，讓讀者不費吹灰之力便能了解實務的運作。

　　不管你是立志海外工作或是在國際公司任職，不論你要留學或出國旅遊，這本書的英文設計讓你能很快的吸收必要的英文知識，使得你在旅行或居住於英語國家時能正確表達出你的想法，讓你英文溝通無礙，且深入了解這些英語國家的餐飲文化。本書不但幫助你英文口語的表達，也讓你建立起英文的信心。

　　本書包含許多不同類型西方餐飲，由漢堡、炸雞等速食店至牛排、下午茶等高檔餐廳。作者精心寫每個單元，由字裡行間我們可以看到作者對於餐飲文化及產業的深入研究，在作者的努力下，才有本書的精采呈現。

　　本書是本務實且嚴謹的教科書／工具書，不管你是四處旅遊的旅行家、觀光飯店產業的專家、學校餐飲課程的教師或者大學餐飲管理的教授、飯店管理人員、學生或自學者，本書絕對是本值得擁有的餐飲英文專書，故樂於推薦之。

許惠峰

許惠峰
中國文化大學法學院 院長及法律學系所主任暨所長
中國文化大學推廣教育部教育長
龐波國際法律事務所 律師／首席資深顧問
美國聖路易華盛頓大學法學博士

FOREWORD

After absorbing the material in English for Food and Beverage Services, I confidently say that it is an absolute "must-have" book. It is very easy to get lost in the tidal waves of books with similar topics flooding the book market. However, it is easy to spot a book that immediately addresses the needs of those in the industry. It fact, it is even a bestseller in its area of specialty.

English in Food and Beverage Services may seem straightforward to some, but as a non-native speaker of English, you well know that it's tough to master. However, you can rest assured that this book will take you through a smooth journey of learning as each unit is carefully cut into bite-sized portions that are easily digested - - it first takes one through a journey of brainstorming, key conversation phrases and mouth-watering pictures that have been carefully selected to represent each unit's essence, and then on to the main conversational piece. The conversations of the book captures the key attributes of the food and beverage services either from a tourist or a tour guide standpoint, allowing one to fully understand what one might actually encounter when placed in a real setting. It is also filled with many practice exercises that enforces one's learning, yet not too taxing.

Whether you aspire to work abroad or in a domestic international setting, wish to travel to or live in an English-speaking country for leisurely or study abroad purposes, this book has been designed to help you quickly and easily absorb what is needed to get there. Its carefully mapped-out units and study design will definitely enable you to master your communications and understanding of what is needed to interact with customers or people in an English-speaking context. This book immediately helps you realize that "speaking" English is not as difficult as it may seem, and will help you gain your confidence in no time.

This book not only enhances your proficiency in spoken English but also fosters confidence in English communication. It encompasses a diverse range of Western and Eastern cuisines, featuring a variety of Western dishes like fried chicken, pizza, high-end steaks, and more, alongside Taiwanese local delicacies such as pearl milk tea and traditional Taiwanese breakfast. from fast food chains such as burgers and fried chicken, to upper-class restaurant settings such as Steakhouses and Afternoon Tea, amongst others. From the way the units are aligned, one immediately knows that the author has displayed major and in-depth research into her work.

This is a no-nonsense textbook/book/handbook, and is already known as a "must-have" whatever youridentity may be - from a world traveler; a professional in the tourism and hospitality, an educator in the College of Food & Beverages, College of Leisure Management, Hospitality Management, College of Business; to a student or self-learner.

Tim Hsu

Professor Tim Hsu (J.S.D)

Dean of Law School, Chinese Culture University

Dean of School of Continuing Education, Chinese Culture University

Attorney-at-Law/Chief Senior Counselor, Washington Group & Associates

J.S.D. Washington University in St. Louis, USA

FOREWORD

　　第一次接觸本書內容時，由我的專業判斷，這是本幫助讀者精通英文口語表達的好書，足以讓讀者學習後，建立起相當的信心面對真實的英文情境。藉由本書的研讀，讀者會發現英文口語表達並不是想像中的困難，對於不是以英文為母語的學習者常覺得英文不是那麼好學，但本書透過口語用法、教學設計及易於吸收的編排方式讓英文學習變得容易。

　　本書每一單元的英文會話情境及場景都非常具有創意，而且是我們真正會遇到的真實情境，作者精心設計使得讀者可以很快的擷取到每一單元的要旨。尤其作者花心思加入同義詞及反義詞，非以英語為母語的讀者常忽略同義詞及反義詞的重要性。如果你有很多國內外旅遊經驗的人，你一定可以立即了解到這本教科書是相當的實務且應用性相當高。

　　本書提供了相當強的實務性及易吸收的內文，使得讀者可以很快的學到真實生活中常用的字彙及片語，直接運用於餐飲產業、觀光及酒店管理的英文會話中。書中包含許多的練習，並以各種形式出現，每一單元學習後，讀者會發現可以不但可以實際運用且能説出正統的英文會話。一旦你研修本書後，我保證你將覺得和餐飲相關的英文溝通已不是障礙。在這些章節中，讀者將學習到許多常見的紅酒名稱，而一些主題和內容還涉及到文化議題，例如台灣夜市文化以及歐美洲豐富多樣的紅白酒文化。這些文化反映了不同地區的歷史、氣候和獨特文化特色，這些內容也在書中呈現，讓讀者不僅學習了語言，還同時深入了解餐飲文化的內涵。因此，本書不光是讓讀者學會英文的溝通能力，也讓讀者習得餐飲文化及禮儀。

　　作者對於餐飲文化及語言有著深入的研究及了解，不論西方餐飲的語言、情境或內容，作者均精心設計，且用心編排各個單元，因對文化及語言的深入，也能知曉非英語國家的學習者常常誤解或遺漏的地方，並在書中導入正確的用法。

　　我衷心推薦這本教科書給予學生及教育工作者，本書相當實務，因此不光是課堂使用的教科書，也是旅遊者、餐飲業管理者及職員必備的好書。

陳迪智
聯合報 教育事業部總經理

FOREWORD

Upon first look at this book, I realize immediately that it will enable you to MASTER & SPEAK English with great confidence when you step into the real English-speaking world. You will find that communications in the English-speaking world, is in fact, not as complicated as one may think. Many non-native speakers of the English language find that English is not an easy language to learn. However, this book is armed with to the point English speaking phrases, proven teaching and learning methods, as well as provides many easy to absorb learning techniques.

Each unit's realistic English-speaking setting is also very creative and brings to life, what one may actually encounter in an actual setting. Such great organization enables one to quickly capture the essences of each unit's contents. The author has also meticulously introduced synonyms as well as antonyms that often throws a non-native speaker of English off-guard. Thus, if you have domestic and international travel experiences, you will also realize that the contents of this textbook are absolutely realistic and immediately applicable.

This book provides a highly effective and efficient resource to teach you words and phrases very commonly used in real-life scenarios in the food and beverage service industry in the English-speaking world of tourism and hospitality management. The book encompasses lots of exercises, repeated in various forms, and by the end of each unit, you will find that you actually CAN ACTUALLY SPEAK English! Once you have gone through the contents of this book, I guarantee that you will have learned an extraordinary range of easy to communicate, English for food and beverages contexts. There are many must-know topics and contents that are included in this textbook such as hard to master red wine and white wine tasting techniques and hard to pronounce, yet the most common wine names. Some topics and content also involve cultural issues, such as Taiwan's night market culture and the rich and diverse red and white wine culture in Europe and America. These cultures reflect the history, climate and unique cultural characteristics of different regions. These contents are also presented in the book, allowing readers to not only learn the language, but also have an in-depth understanding of the connotation of catering culture. Therefore, this book not only allows readers to learn English communication skills, but also allows readers to acquire catering culture and etiquette.

The author shows a great amount of depth in understanding in culture and language used in the Food & Beverage Service industry – the language, scenarios and contexts used in Western cultures that are often missed out or misunderstood by a non-native speaker – have all been carefully hand-picked and embedded into the contents of each unit. I highly recommend this book as it is not only practical, but realistic. Whether it's for classroom usage, travelers, managers or employees in the, this is definitely a must have book in your bookshelf.

Chen, Steven Ti-Chih

General Manager of Education Department, United Daily News Group

　　本書適用於以英文為第二語言的學習者，符合各類餐旅從業人員、留學者、遊學者及證照考試等英文學習需求。亦可用於大專院校的餐飲學系、休閒管理系、商用英文等課程教科書，且可滿足遊學者、留學者、餐飲業、國際導遊證照、國內導遊證照、度假工讀 (Working Holiday Programs) 之實務應用，適於各類服務業及經常出國旅遊的人。

　　本書模仿實際餐飲的流程及處理程序，涉入餐飲服務重要的細節，使讀者能契合實際狀況來學習。例如模仿客戶點餐、甜點及買單等不同情境，並強調其間不同的做法及意義，如西式晚餐或下午茶的差異，或在咖啡廳和酒吧點酒的差異。

　　通常非英美人士聽到以前沒有學過的英文用法時，即使語意相近，通常仍不了解別人所要表達的意思。因此，我搜集了常用的字彙及片語，故即使非英美人士聽到這類的詞彙，也能有所意會，例如：”host/hostess” 也就是我們所熟知男侍者及女侍者” waiter/waitress” 的意思；而”jumbo” 是超大 “extra large” 的意思。此外，本書以系統性的方法介紹同義字詞，免於被一大堆相似字詞淹沒，例如在第一章我們會先介紹女侍者 hostess 這個詞彙，後面章節我們會介紹服務生 server 詞彙，些詞彙意思均相近，但是卻會被運用於不同的情境。

鄭寶菁

Brainstorming 腦力激盪

列出本章重點單字，提供學生課前簡單預習，可讓學生自由挑選最想要的選項，並於課堂討論。

Conversation 會話

模擬餐飲行業之實境會話，增進英語溝通能力。

New Words & Phrases 單字及片語

QRCODE 真人語音發音，隨掃隨聽，單字發音練習好簡單！

Key Words 重點單字

圖像記憶學習法，輔以圖片增加印象，讓枯燥的背誦單字更簡單。

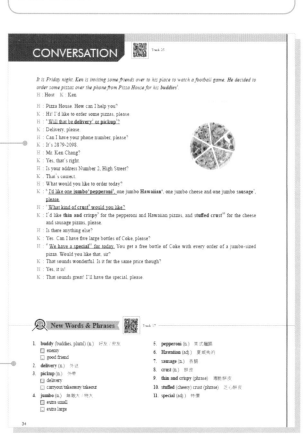

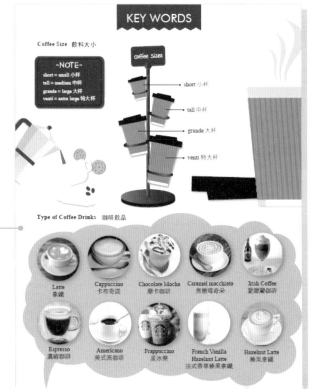

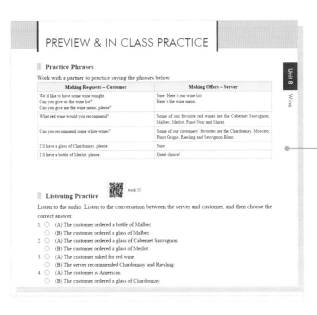

PREVIEW & IN CLASS PRACTICE
會話預習

會話前的預習加速進入學習狀況，有效提升上課之學習成效。

Important Speaking Practice Exercise
重要句子練習

節錄單元重要句子，有助於提升聽力及口說能力，貼近生活，可應用於飯店、旅遊及餐飲等場所。

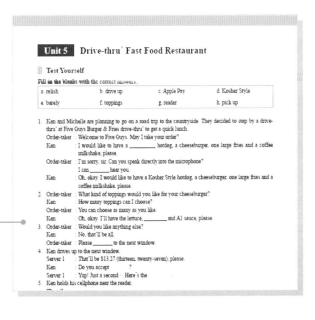

HOMEWORK EXERCISES 課後練習

藉由練習題不斷強化及反覆練習前面所學習之大量口說英語、聽力內容、關鍵詞彙、重要句子和行業關鍵詞，以達到事半功倍之學習效果。

CONTENTS

Unit 1

Learning Objectives

What you will learn in this unit…
- How to make a restaurant reservation as a customer?
- How to take a restaurant reservation from a customer?
- Types of restaurant seating areas.
- About corkage fees or BYOW – Bring Your Own Wine charges.
- Types of restaurants such as fine dining, bistros, etc.
- Restaurant reservation related keyword verbs, phrases and idioms.

Brainstorming

Where do you like to be seated in a restaurant, and what does it say about you?

☐ By the window / 靠窗

☐ By the fountain or near the fountain area
坐在噴泉旁或靠近噴泉

☐ By the patio / 坐在庭院

☐ At the bar area / 坐在吧台

☐ In a private room / VIP room / booth
坐在包廂內

1. What is your favorite restaurant type? (Example: bistro.)
2. Ask your partner what are three restaurant types that he/she likes, and the name of those restaurants. Example: hotpot restaurant (Mala Hotpot).
3. What are some examples of ethnic restaurants in Taiwan? (Example: Japanese.)

KEY WORDS

takeout / takeaway
外帶

food delivery (Uber Eats / Foodpanda)
食物外送

drive-thru'
得來速

food truck
餐車

fine dining restaurant
精緻餐飲

outdoor dining
戶外用餐

fast food restaurant
(KFC, McDonald's)
速食店

casual dining restaurant
休閒餐廳

PREVIEW & IN CLASS PRACTICE

Practice Phrases

Work with a partner to practice saying the phrases below.

Host/ Hostess	Customer
• Good evening, sir/ma'am. • This is Bubba Gum's restaurant. This is Samantha. • How may I help you?	• Yes, I'd like to make a reservation.
• When would you like to make reservation for?	• July 2nd. • 2nd of July.
• What time will that be?	• 7:30 p.m. • 7:30 in the evening.
• How many in your party?	• Ten. • There are ten of us.
• Is there anything else I can help you with?	• Yes. Can we have a private room, please? • I'd like to request for a VIP room, please? • I'd like a private area, please.
• Just give me a moment, please. • Let me check. • Please hold the line.	• Sure.
• Yes, we have a private room available for July 2nd at 7:30 p.m.	• That sounds great! • That's great!
• Anything else I can help you with?	• Yes. We will be celebrating one of our friend's birthday on that day. • So, I was wondering if we could bring our own wine?
• We charge a corkage fee of $10 per bottle of wine.	• Ok, got it!
• Anything else I can help you with?	• No, that'll be all.

Listening Practice

 Track 01

Listen to the audio. Listen to the conversation between the hostess and the customer, and then choose the correct answer.

1. ○ (A) The name of the restaurant is Bubba Gum restaurant.

   ○ (B) The name of the restaurant is Amy's restaurant.

2. ○ (A) The customer is making a reservation for six people.

   ○ (B) The customer wishes to party at the restaurant with six people.

3. ○ (A) The customer would like a private room.

   ○ (B) The customer is a private person.

4. ○ (A) The customer will be charged $10 for bringing each bottle of wine.

   ○ (B) The customer will be not be charged for $10 for bringing each bottle of wine.

CONGVERSATION

Track 02

*Ken wants to **make a reservation**[1] for ten at Bubba Gum's restaurant.*

H：Hostess[2]　　K：Ken

H : Good afternoon, Bubba Gum restaurant. This is Samantha. How may I help you?

K : Yes, I'd like to make a **reservation**[3].

H : Sure. [a] When would you like to make reservation for?

K : July 2nd

H : Alright. What time will that be?

K : Seven-thirty in the evening (7:30).

H : [b] How many in your **party**[4]?

K : Ten.

H : Ok. [c] Is there **anything else**[5] I can help you with?

K : Can I have a private room, please?

H : Just give me a moment, please. Let me check. [d] Please hold the line.

K : Sure.

H : Yes, we have a **private room**[6] available for July 2nd at 7:30 p.m.

K : That sounds great!

*The hostess is **confirming**[7] some information for Ken's reservation for July 2nd.*

H : Can I have your name and **cellphone**[8] number, please?

K : Sure. My name is Ken Jordan, and my cellphone number is 0983-112-310.

H : Okay, Mr. Jordan. We have a private room for ten at 7:30 p.m. on July 2nd. Is that correct?

K : Yes, that's right.

H : [e] We will **hold your reservation**[9] for fifteen minutes. Please arrive before 7:15 p.m.

K : Sure. I'll be there before 7:15.

H : Anything else I can help you with?

K : Yes. We will be celebrating one of our friend's birthday on that day. So, I was wondering if we could bring our own wine?

H : [f] We charge a **corkage fee**[10] of $10 per bottle of wine.

 New Words & Phrases Track 03

1. **make a reservation** (n.)　預定 / 預約 / 保留
   同 Make an arrangement
   反 Cancel a reservation

2. **hostess** (n.)　女侍者
   同 waitress　　反 host / waiter

3. **reservation** (n.)　預定 / 預約 / 保留
   同 booking

4. **party** (n.)　一夥人

5. **anything else** (Idiom)　還有其他嗎？
   同 Is that all?

6. **private room** (n.)　包廂
   同 In a booth / VIP room / private section / private area / private section
   反 In an open area / At a food court)

7. **confirm** (v.)　確認
   同 guarantee　　反 deny

8. **cellphone** (n.)　手機
   同 hand phone / mobile phone / cell
   反 landline / telephone line

9. **hold your reservation** (phrase)　保留你的訂位
   同 keep your reservation
   反 Cancel a reservation

10. **corkage fee** (n.)
    （飯店對自帶酒水收取的）開瓶費
    同 Bring Your Own Wine (BYOW)) / cover charge
    反 No corkage fees

K : Ok, got it!

H : Anything else I can help you with?

K : No, that'll be all.

H : Ok. Mr. Jordan. [g] We will call you a day before to confirm your reservation.

K : That'll be great!

H : [h] **Look forward to seeing you!**

Important!

Speaking Practice Exercise

Practice saying the below short sentences.

a. When would you like to make a reservation for?
你想預訂那一天呢？

b. How many in your party? (How many people in your group?)
請問有幾位呢？

c. Is there anything else?
您還需要什麼嗎？

d. Please hold the line.
請稍等。

e. We will hold your reservation for fifteen minutes.
您的訂位我們會為您保留 15 分鐘。

f. We charge a corkage fee of $10 per bottle of wine.
我們每一瓶葡萄酒的開瓶費是十美元。

g. We will call you a day before to confirm your reservation.
我們會在前一天打電話給您，確認您的定位。

h. Look forward to seeing you!
期待見到您！

Q & A

1. What is the name of the hostess who answered Ken's call?

_____

2. How many people did Ken make a reservation for?

_____

3. What kind of room did Ken request for?

_____

4. What time does Ken have to arrive at the restaurant?

_____

5. What is the corkage fee at Bubba Gum restaurant for a bottle of wine?

_____

Listening Practice

Track 04

Listen to the conversation and fill in the blanks.

1. The customer would like to make a _____ for July _____.
2. The customer is making a reservation for _____ people.
3. The customer requested for a _____ _____ .
4. The customer will be charged a _____ _____ of $10 per bottle of wine.
5. The hostess will call the customer _____ day before his reservation date.

Match the pictures with the words given below

a. "Please hold the line"

b. private room / VIP room / booth / private area / private section

c. You can BYOW (Bring Your Own Wine) / No Corkage Fees

d. cellphone / hand phone / mobile phone / cell

e. hostess

f. A party of seven

1. _____

2. _____

3. _____

4. _____

5. _____

6. _____

Listen and Pronounce

Track 05

Listen to each of the following types of restaurants/eateries and try pronouncing each one of them.

• Bakery Café 麵包咖啡廳	• Barbecue Restaurant（BBQ） 燒烤	• Bistro 小酒館
• Cafeteria 自助餐廳	• Café 咖啡館	• Casual Dining Restaurants 休閒餐廳
• Drive-thru' 得來速	• Ethnic Restaurants 多元種族餐廳	← **Examples:** Italian restaurant　意大利餐廳 Vietnamese restaurant　越南餐廳

Examples:

• Fast food restaurant 　速食店 　（例如：KFC, McDonald's）	• Fine dining restaurant 　精緻餐飲	• Food Delivery 　食物外送 　（Uber Eats / Foodpanda）
• Food Truck 　餐車	• Hotdog Stand 　熱狗小販	• Hotpot Restaurant 　火鍋店
• Outdoor Dining 　戶外用餐	• Sandwich Bar 　三明治專賣店	• Steakhouses 　牛排館
• Street Food 　路邊攤 / 街頭美食	• Takeout / Takeaway 　外帶	• Teppanyaki Restaurant 　鐵板燒餐廳

Photographs

1. Choose the sentence that best describes the picture.

(A) A party of ten friends are making a reservation at a restaurant.
(B) A party of ten friends are celebrating a birthday party together.
(C) A party of six friends are celebrating a birthday party together.
(D) A party of six friends are being charged a corkage fee for drinking wine.

Your answer: (　　)

2. Choose the sentence that best describes the picture.

(A) Some people are celebrating a birthday party and having dinner in a public area at a restaurant.
(B) Some people are celebrating a birthday party and having dinner in a private room at a restaurant.
(C) Some people are celebrating a birthday party and having dinner near a fountain area at a restaurant.
(D) Some people are celebrating a birthday party and having dinner at a patio in a restaurant.

Your answer: (　　)

 **In-Class Role Play**

Practice Role Play Exercise 1

- Using the below short conversation, ask each student to find a partner to practice with. One student plays the role of hostess (H), and the other, the customer (C).
- Then, change roles.

Practice Role Play Exercise 2

1. Now, practice again.
2. This time, replace the underlined words with your own words.
3. Replace the Month / Day using the charts given below:

   CHART A: Months of the year

   CHART B: Dates ordinal numbers

   Example: January 1st.

4. Replace the time using the chart given below:

   CHART C: Illustration of a clock with time

   Examples:

   7:30 am

   12:00 pm / noon

   6:30 pm

5. Replace the type of seating using the chart given below:

   CHART D: Types of seating

   Example: booth.

Chart A: Months of the Year

Chart B: Dates Ordinal Numbers

1	2	3	4	5	6	7	8	9	10
1st	2nd	3rd	4th	5th	6th	7th	8th	9th	10th
11	12	13	14	15	16	17	18	19	20
11th	12th	13th	14th	15th	16th	17th	18th	19th	20th
21	22	23	24	25	26	27	28	29	30
21st	22nd	23rd	24th	25th	26th	27th	28th	29th	30th
31									
31st									

Chart C: Illustration of a Clock with Time

Midnight=12:00 at night

Noon=12:00 in the day

Chart D: Types of Seating

1. by the window
2. by the fountain area
3. near the fountain area
4. by the patio
5. at the bar
6. in a quiet area
7. in the non-smoking section / area
8. in the smoking section / area
9. in a private room / private area / private section / booth / VIP room
10. outdoors

SHORT CONVERSATION PRACTICE

C : **Customer** 客戶

H : **Hostess** 女服務生

- -

H : Good <u>afternoon</u>, <u>Bubba Gum</u> restaurant. This is <u>Samantha</u>. How may I help you?

C : Yes, I'd like to make a reservation.

H : Sure. When would you like to make reservation for?

C : <u>July 2nd</u>.

H : Alright. What time will that be?

C : <u>Seven-thirty in the evening (7:30)</u>.

H : How many in your party?

C : <u>Ten</u>.

H : Ok. Is there anything else I can help you with?

C : Can I be seated <u>in a private room</u>, please?

H : Just give me a moment, please. Let me check. Please hold the line.

C : Sure.

H : Yes, we have a <u>private room</u> available for <u>July 2nd</u> at <u>7:30 p.m</u>.

C : That sounds great!

Unit 2

Fried Chicken
炸雞

Learning Objectives

What you will learn in this unit…
- How to serve fried chicken at a fast food restaurant.
- How to order fried chicken at a fast food restaurant.
- Fried chicken fast food restaurant related keyword verbs, phrases and idioms.
- Fried chicken fast food restaurant menu items.

Brainstorming

Which is your favorite fried chicken (fast food) restaurant? And, what does it say about you?

☐ Fat Old Daddy / 胖老爹

☐ Dicos / 德克士

☐ Kentucky Fried Chicken
肯德基

☐ T.K.K.
Fried Chicken / 頂呱呱

☐ Rangers Fried Chicken
德州美墨炸雞

1. What parts of the chicken do you like?
   (Examples: drumsticks, wings or breasts, etc.)
2. How do you like your chicken?
   (Examples: original, spicy, grilled, BBQ, crispy, etc.)
3. Ask your partner what part of the chicken he/she likes, and what is his/her favorite fried chicken fast food restaurant?

Family Meal / Bucket Meal 全家餐／雞塊桶

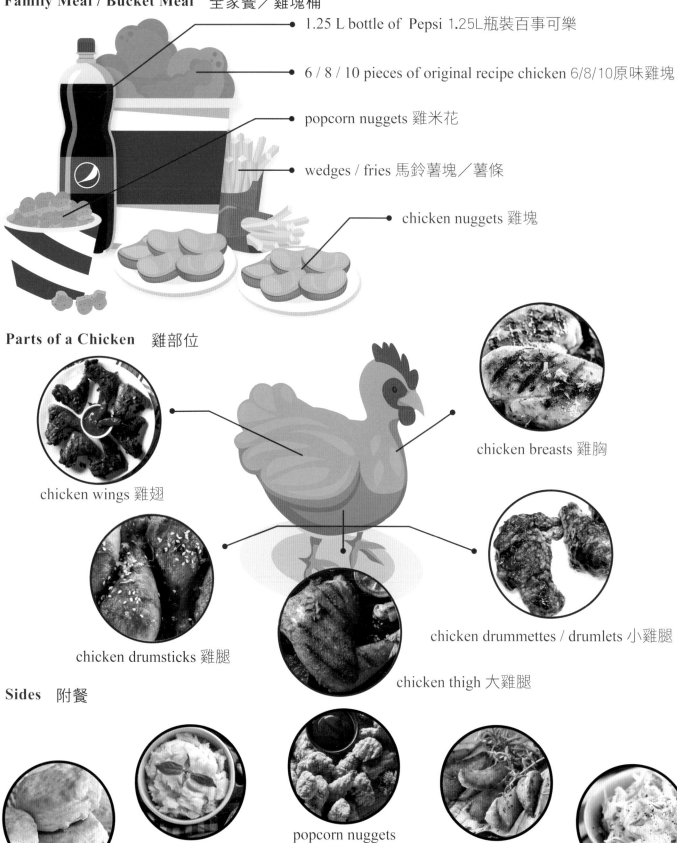

1.25 L bottle of Pepsi 1.25L瓶裝百事可樂

6 / 8 / 10 pieces of original recipe chicken 6/8/10原味雞塊

popcorn nuggets 雞米花

wedges / fries 馬鈴薯塊／薯條

chicken nuggets 雞塊

Parts of a Chicken 雞部位

chicken wings 雞翅

chicken breasts 雞胸

chicken drumsticks 雞腿

chicken drummettes / drumlets 小雞腿

chicken thigh 大雞腿

Sides 附餐

biscuits
比司吉

mashed potatoes
馬鈴薯泥

popcorn nuggets
雞米花

wedges
馬鈴薯條／塊

coleslaw
涼拌卷心菜

PREVIEW & IN CLASS PRACTICE

Practice Phrases

Work with a partner to practice saying the phrases below.

Making Offers – Server	Making Requests – Customer
Can I take your order?	Yes. I'd like to have ten pieces of chicken, please. I'd like to have an eight-piece family meal, please. I'd like to have a coleslaw and a large Coke, please.
Would you like to try our family meal? Would you like to try our bucket meal?	That sounds great! How many pieces of chicken are there in the family meal? How many pieces of chicken are there in a bucket meal?
Would you like our original or spicy recipe? Would you like our original or crispy recipe? Would you like our original or barbecue recipe? Would you like our Mexican or Teriyaki recipe?	Original recipe, please. Spicy, please. Crispy recipe, please. Barbecue (BBQ), please.
What kind of sides would you like? You can choose two sides. What would you like?	Popcorn nuggets, please. Coleslaw, please. Biscuits, please. Mashed potatoes, please. Wedges, please. Mashed potatoes and wedges, please.
What would you like to drink?	I'd like a Coke, please. Coke, please. A large Coke, please. Can I have a bottle of Coke, please?

Listening Practice track 06

Listen to the audio. Listen to the conversation between the hostess and customer, and then choose the correct answer.

1. ○ (A) The customer would like to order a family meal.
   ○ (B) The customer would like to order eight pieces of chicken.
2. ○ (A) The customer would like a cold sore.
   ○ (B) The customer would like a coleslaw.
3. ○ (A) The customer wants to play drums.
   ○ (B) The customer wants to order drumsticks.
4. ○ (A) The customer wants the original recipe.
   ○ (B) The customer wants the spicy recipe.

*Ken was feeling **famished**[1] after a good game of badminton with Jason, his best friend. They were so hungry that they decided to get some fried chicken at KKFC.*

K : Ken   J : Jason   S : Server

K : What would you like to have, Jason?

J : **The usual**[2].

K : Ok. I'll go and order. Why don't you find a table for us?

J : Ok, sure!

*Ken walked over to the **counter**[3] while Jason went to look for a table.*

S : Next! Can I take your order?

K : Yes. I'd like to have ten pieces of chicken, one large **coleslaw**[4] and two large Cokes, please.

S : **In that case**[5], [a] would you like to try our **family meal**[6] instead? It comes with ten pieces of chicken, two **sides**[7] and two large drinks. [b] You get more **value**[8] this way.

K : That sounds great! But, can I have five **drumsticks**[9] and five chicken **wings**[10], please?

S : Sure. [c] Would you like our **original**[11] or **spicy**[12] **recipe**[13]?

K : Spicy, please.

S : [d] What kind of sides would you like?

K : Coleslaw and **popcorn nuggets**[14] please.

S : Ok. What would you like to drink?

K : Coke, please. [e] Are the drinks **refillable**[15]?

S : Yes. You may refill by the **soda fountain**[16] right by the corner.

 New Words & Phrases Track 08

1. **famish** (v.) 挨餓
   同 very hungry
   反 full
2. **the usual** (adj.) 跟平常一樣
3. **counter** (n.) 櫃檯
4. **coleslaw** (n.) 涼拌卷心菜
5. **in that case** (phrase) 如果是那樣的話
6. **family meal** (n.) 全家餐
   反 bucket meal
7. **sides** (n.) 配菜 / 配餐 / 小菜
8. **value** (n.) 超值 / 計算價格 / 重要性 / 價格
9. **chicken drumstick** (n.) 雞腿
   同 chicken leg
   反 chicken drumlets/drummettes

10. **chicken wings** (n.) 雞翅
11. **original** (adj.) 原味
12. **spicy** (adj.) 辣味
    反 non-spicy
13. **recipe** (n.) 食譜 / 製作
    同 flavor
14. **popcorn nuggets** (n.) 雞米花
15. **refillable** (adj.) 可續杯的
    反 non-refillable
16. **soda fountain** (n.) 冷飲櫃 / 汽水龍頭 (供應汽水的裝置)

K : That sounds great!

S : Anything else I can help you with?

K : No, that's it.

S : For here or to go?

K : For here.

S : Your total comes up to $35.70.

K : Here you go. Here's forty.

S : Four thirty ($4.30) is your change.

K : Thank you.

S : Have a nice day.

Q & A

1. What did Ken and Steven do before they went to KKFC?

   _____

2. What was the reason that they wanted to go to KKFC?

   _____

3. What did Ken want to order initially?

   _____

4. What did the server recommend to Ken?

   _____

5. What did Ken decide to choose from the side menu?

   _____

Important!
Speaking Practice Exercise

a. Would you like to try our family meal?
   你要試試看我們的全家餐嗎？

b. You get more value this way.
   這樣比較便宜 (划算)。

c. Would you like our original or spicy recipe?
   請問你要原味或辣味？

d. What kind of sides would you like?
   你要什麼配菜呢？

e. Are the drinks refillable?
   飲料可以續杯嗎？

Vocabulary Review

Antonym

1. spicy: _____
2. chicken drumstick: _____
3. famished: _____
4. refillable: _____

Synonym

1. recipe: _____
2. family meal: _____
3. very hungry: _____
4. for here: _____

Match the Pictures

Match the pictures to the answers given below.

a. popcorn nuggets	b. refill (soda fountain)	c. mashed potatoes
d. chicken drumsticks	e. chicken drummettes	f. biscuits
g. coleslaw	f. chicken wings	

1. _____

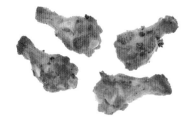

2. _____

3. _____

4. _____

5. _____

6. _____

7. _____

8. _____

What's in your family meal?

Create your own family meal.

Example:

<u>Original</u> recipe, <u>3 chicken drumsticks</u>, <u>3 chicken wings</u>, <u>2 coleslaw</u>, <u>2 corn</u> and a bottle of Pepsi.

Chicken recipe   chicken parts   chicken parts   sides   sides
(I)   (II)   (II)   (III)   (III)

(I) Chicken Recipe / Flavors 雞肉口味

- Crispy 脆皮
- Original 原味
- Spicy 辛辣
- Grilled 燒烤

(II) Parts of a Chicken 雞部位

- Chicken breast 雞胸
- Chicken wing 雞翅
- Chicken thigh 大雞腿
- Chicken drumstick 雞腿
- Chicken drummettes / drumlets 小棒棒腿

(III) Sides 附餐

- Biscuits 比司吉
- Coleslaw 涼拌卷心菜
- Macaroni & cheese 起司通心麵
- Mashed potatoes 馬鈴薯泥
- Popcorn nuggets 雞米花
- Wedges/ Fries 馬鈴薯條 / 塊
- Kernel corn 玉米粒

1. _____recipe, <u>3 chicken</u> _____, <u>3 chicken</u> _____, 2 _____, 2 _____ and a bottle of Pepsi.

Chicken recipe   chicken parts   chicken parts   sides   sides
(I)   (II)   (II)   (III)   (III)

2. _____recipe, <u>3 chicken</u> _____, <u>3 chicken</u> _____, 2 _____, 2 _____ and a bottle of Pepsi.

Chicken recipe   chicken parts   chicken parts   sides   sides
(I)   (II)   (II)   (III)

3. _____recipe, <u>3 chicken</u> _____, <u>3 chicken</u> _____, 2 _____, 2 _____ and a bottle of Pepsi.

Chicken recipe   chicken parts   chicken parts   sides   sides
(I)   (II)   (II)   (III)   (III)

4. _____recipe, <u>3 chicken</u> _____, <u>3 chicken</u> _____, 2 _____, 2 _____ and a bottle of Pepsi.

Chicken recipe   chicken parts   chicken parts   sides   sides
(I)   (II)   (II)   (III)   (III)

Vocabulary Review

Match the questions to the answers below.

a. refillable	b. sides	c. to go
d. value	e. anything else	

1. C: I'd like eight pieces of drumsticks, please.

   S: For here or _____?

2. S: Would you like to try our family meal? It is cheaper than just ordering eight pieces of drumsticks. You get more _____ this way.

3. S: What kind of _____ would you like?

   C: I'd like mashed potatoes, please.

4. C: Are the drinks _____?

   S: Yes, there's a soda fountain right over there.

5. S: Would you like _____?

   C: No, that'll be all.

 track 09

Listen and Pronounce

Listen to the audio first. Then, try pronouncing each one of the menu items below.

Chicken Flavors	Sides/Side Menu/Side	
• Crispy 脆的	• Biscuits 比司吉	• Popcorn nuggets 雞米花
• Original recipe 原味作法	• Coleslaw 涼拌卷心菜	• Wedges 馬鈴薯條 / 塊
• Spicy 辛辣的	• Macaroni & cheese 起司通心麵	• Kernel corn 玉米粒
• Grilled 烤的	• Mashed potatoes 馬鈴薯泥	

Photographs

Look at the picture below and then try to name the items.

a. coleslaw	b. original recipe chicken	c. two bottles of Pepsi
d. mashed potatoes	e. wedges / fries	

In-Class Role Play

Firstly, place the below sentences in the correct order. Then, using your answers, practice the conversation. One student plays the role of server, and the other, the customer. Using the below menu, try to order different types of items. Replace the underlined words with different items on the menu. Practice as many times as possible, ordering different items from each menu above, and changing roles.

(   ) 1.   Can I have <u>mashed potatoes</u> and <u>biscuits,</u> please?

(   ) 2.   Sure. And, what would you like to drink?

(   ) 3.   I'd like to have a <u>ten-piece</u> family meal, please.

(   ) 4.   Sure. Would you like our <u>original</u> or spicy recipe?

(   ) 5.   <u>Spicy,</u> please.

(   ) 6.   You can choose two sides. What would you like?

(   ) 7.   <u>No, that's it.</u>

(   ) 8   Is this for here or to go?

(   ) 9.   <u>For here,</u> please.

(   ) 10. Your total comes up to <u>$16.90</u>.

(   ) 11. <u>Coke,</u> please.

(   ) 12. Anything else I can help you with?

(   ) 13.   Next! Can I take your order?

Chicken Recipes

Original Recipe

Crispy Recipe

Grilled Recipe

Family Meals

8 Pc. Meal with 2 Large Sides & 4 Biscuits	$21.99
8 Pc. Chicken Only	$14.99
12 Pc. Meal with 3 Large Sides & 6 Biscuits	$29.99
12 Pc. Chicken Only	$20.49
16 Pc. Meal with 4 Large Sides & 8 Biscuits	$36.99
16 Pc. Chicken Only	$24.99

Drinks

Hot tea	$2.59
Iced tea	$2.49
Lemonade	$1.99
Bottled water	$1.69
Americano	$2.49
Cappuccino	$3.05
Pepsi	Small $0.99 Medium $1.49 Large $1.89
7-Up	Small $0.99 Medium $1.49 Large $1.89

Sides

Individual $1.59   Large $2.99

Mashed Potatoes

Popcorn Nuggets

Coleslaw

Biscuits

Potato Wedges

Sweet Com

Unit 3

Traditional Taiwanese Breakfast
傳統台灣早餐

 Learning Objectives

What you will learn in this unit…
- How to serve Taiwanese traditional breakfast.
- How to order Taiwanese traditional breakfast.
- Names of different Taiwanese traditional breakfast foods.
- Names of different Taiwanese traditional breakfast drinks.
- Traditional Taiwanese breakfast related keyword verbs, phrases and idioms.

 Brainstorming

What kind of traditional Taiwanese breakfast you like tells about you?

☐ Steamed bun (with egg)
饅頭（夾蛋）

☐ Taiwanese congee and side dishes
清粥小菜

☐ Twisted cruller / fried bread
油條

☐ Salted soymilk 鹹豆漿

☐ Clay oven roll (with /without egg)
燒餅夾蛋

1. What kind of Taiwanese traditional breakfast drinks have you had before?
   (Example: soybean milk, Taiwanese milk tea, etc.)
2. What kind of Taiwanese traditional breakfast items have you had before?
   (Example: fried turnip bun, steamed bun with egg, etc.)
3. What is your favorite Taiwanese traditional breakfast item, and why?
4. Ask your partner what breakfast items she/he likes?

Traditioal Taiwanese breakfast 臺式早餐

turnip cake / radish cake
蘿蔔糕
with thick soy sauce /
with chili sauce
加醬油膏／加辣椒

Taiwanese sweet
glutinous rice roll
紫米飯糰

Taiwanese omelet
蛋餅
with thick soy sauce
加醬油膏

thin green onion cake
with twisted cruller
煎餅油條

steamed pork bun
in a bamboo steamer
(10 pieces)
一籠小籠湯包(10粒)

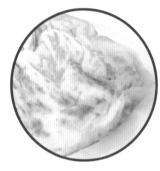

flaky scallion pancake
蔥抓餅

hot / cold soybean milk
熱／冰豆漿

rice and peanut milk
米漿

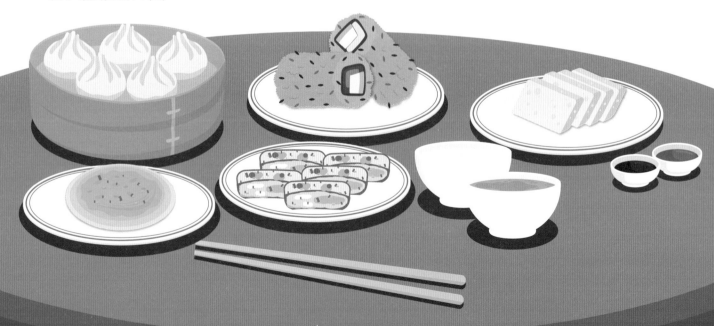

PREVIEW & IN CLASS PRACTICE

Practice Phrases

Work with a partner to practice saying the phrases below.

Server	Customer
• Good morning. Are you ready to order?	• Yes, I am. I'll have and turnip cake with thick soy sauce and chili sauce, please.
• Would you like to add an egg?	• Yes, please.
• Would you like anything to drink?	• I'll have a hot soybean milk, please. • A hot rice & peanut milk, please. • A hot milk tea, please.
• Is that all?	• Yes, that'd be all.
• Your total will be fifty five dollars, please.	• Here you go.
• Would you like any cutlery?	• A pair of chopsticks and a straw, please. • A pair of chopsticks, please. • A straw, please. • No, thanks.
• Sure. Here's your change.	• Thank you.

Listening Practice

Track 10

Listen to the audio. Listen to the conversation between the server/cashier and the customer, and then choose the correct answer.

1. ○ (A) The customer would like to order a bowl of rice.
   ○ (B) The customer would like to order a Taiwanese sweet glutinous rice roll.
2. ○ (A) The customer would like to order a hot rice and peanut milk.
   ○ (B) The customer wants like to order a soybean milk.
3. ○ (A) The total price of the breakfast is one hundred dollars.
   ○ (B) The total price of the breakfast is sixty dollars.
4. ○ (A) The customer requested for a pair of straws and chopsticks.
   ○ (B) The customer requested for a pair of chopsticks and a straw.

23

CONSERVATION

 Track 11

On Saturday morning, Ken, Michelle and Penny decided to have a local breakfast together. They visited a local Taiwanese breakfast shop, called Soy Milk Shop.

S：Server　K：Ken　W：Waitress　C：Cashier　M：Michelle　P：Penny

S ：Good morning. Are you ready to order?

K ：Yes. Can I have a **turnip cake with thick soy sauce and chili sauce,**[1] please.

S ：[a] Would you like to add an egg?

K ：Yes, please.

S ：Would you like anything to drink?

K ：I'll have a **hot soybean milk**[2], please.

W ：Is that all?

K ：Yes, that'd be all.

C ：[b] Your total will be fifty five dollars, please.

K ：Here you go.

C ：[c] Would you like any **cutlery**[3]?

K ：[d] A pair of chopsticks and a straw, please.

C ：Sure. [e] Here's your **change**[4].

Michelle was next in line.

S ：What can I get for you, ma'am?

M ：I'll have a **Taiwanese sweet glutinous**[5] **rice**[6] **roll**[7], please.

W ：[f] Will that be all?

M ：Can I have a **hot rice & peanut milk**[8], please?

W ：Of course. Will that be all?

M ：[g] Yes, that's it for now. Thank you.

C ：Your total will be sixty dollars, please.

M ：Here's $100.

C ：Would you like any cutlery?

M ：No, thanks.

C ：[h] Thirty-five dollars is your change.

New Words & Phrases

 Track 12

1. **turnip cake with thick soy sauce and chili sauce**
   (n.) 蘿蔔糕（加辣椒／加醬油膏）
   同 radish cake

2. **hot soybean milk** (n.) 熱豆漿
   反 cold soybean milk

3. **cutlery** (n.) 餐具／餐飲用具
   Examples: chopsticks 筷子, straw 吸管,
   　　　　　 spoon 湯匙.
   同 eating utensils / tableware

4. **change** (n.) 找零錢
   同 coin 反 notes

5. **glutinous** (adj.) 黏的／黏質的
   同 sticky 反 syrupy

6. **glutinous rice** (n.) 糯米
   同 sticky rice

7. **Taiwanese sweet glutinous rice roll** 紫米飯糰
   同 Taiwanese sweet sticky rice roll

8. **Rice & peanut milk** (n.) 米漿

24

Turning to Penny, the server asked for her order.

S : Good morning. May I take your order?

P : I'll have a **Taiwanese omelet**[9.] please.

S : [i] Would you like some sauce to go along with it?

P : Some **chili sauce**[10] and **soy sauce**[11] would be great.

S : Anything to drink?

P : [j] Can I have a hot milk tea, please?

S : Anything else?

P : No, that'll be all. Thanks.

C : Would you like any cutlery?

M : A pair of chopsticks and a straw, please.

C : Sure. You total will be sixty-five dollars, please.

P : Here you are.

Q & A

1. What is the name of the local Taiwanese breakfast shop that Ken, Michelle and Penny visited on one Saturday morning?

   _____

2. What did Ken order?

   _____

3. How much is Michelle's breakfast?

   _____

4. What did Penny order?

   _____

5. What cutlery did Penny ask for?

   _____

Important!
Speaking Practice Exercise

Practice saying the below short sentences.

a. Would you like to add an egg?
   你要加蛋嗎？

b. Your total will be fifty five dollars, please.
   總共是五十五元。

c. Would you like any cutlery?
   你需要餐具嗎？

d. A pair of chopsticks and a straw, please.
   請給我一雙筷子，還有一根吸管。

e. Here's your change.
   這是找你的零錢。

f. Will that be all?
   你還要加點什麼嗎？

g. Yes, that's it for now. Thank you!
   是的，就這樣。謝謝！

h. Thirty-five dollars is your change.
   找你三十五美元。

i. Would you like some sauce to go along with it?
   你要加醬料嗎？

j. Can I have a hot milk tea, please?
   請給我一杯熱奶茶？

---

 9. **Taiwanese omelet** (n.)　蛋餅
10. **chili sauce** (n.)　辣椒醬
    同 tabasco sauce / hot sauce
    反 sweet sauce
11. **soy sauce** (n.)　醬油

Listening Practice

Track 13

Listen to the conversation and fill in the blanks using the answers given below:

1. The customer ordered a Taiwanese _____ with chili sauce and soy sauce.

2. The customer ordered a hot _____ _____.

3. The cashier asked if the customer would like any _____.

4. The total price of the breakfast is _____-_____ dollars.

Picture-Vocabulary Review

Match the pictures to the answers below:

a. soy bean milk

b. soy sauce and chili sauce

c. turnip cake with thick soy sauce and chili sauce

d. cutlery

e. change

f. Taiwanese glutinous rice roll

1. _____

2. _____

3. _____

4. _____

5. _____

6. _____

Listen and Pronounce

Track 14

Listen to the audio first. Then, try practice pronouncing each one of the Taiwanese breakfast food and drinks below:

Taiwanese Breakfast Food

• Clay oven roll (with or without egg) 燒餅 (夾蛋 / 不要夾蛋)	• Flaky scallion pancake 蔥抓餅
• Pork bun 肉包	• Vegetable bun 菜包
• Turnip cake / Radish cake (with thick soy sauce / with chili sauce) 蘿蔔糕（加醬油膏 / 加辣椒）	• Steamed pork buns in a bamboo steamer (10 pieces) 一龍小籠湯包（10 粒）
• Scallion pancake 蔥油餅	• Steamed bun (with or without egg) 饅頭（夾蛋 / 不要夾蛋）
• Taiwanese sweet glutinous rice roll 紫米飯糰	• Taiwanese glutinous rice roll 飯糰
• Sweet potato congee 地瓜稀飯	• Taiwanese omelet 蛋餅
• Thin green onion cake with twisted cruller 煎餅油條	• Twisted cruller / fried breadstick 油條
• Salted soymilk 鹹豆漿	

Taiwanese Breakfast Drinks

• Hot / Cold Soybean Milk 熱 / 冰 豆漿	• Rice & Peanut Milk 米漿	• Hot / Cold Milk Tea 熱 / 冰 奶茶

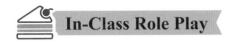 **In-Class Role Play**

Practice Role Play Exercise 1

- Using the below short conversation, ask each student to find a partner to practice with. One student plays the role of server (S), and the other, the customer (C).
- Then, change roles.

Practice Role Play Exercise 2

- Now, practice again. This time, using the below menu, ask the students to replace the <u>underlined words</u> with items from the menu.

SHORT CONVERSATION PRACTICE

C : Customer 客戶   S : Server 服務生

. . . .

S : Good morning. May I take your order?

C : I'll have a <u>Taiwanese omelet</u> please.

S : Would you like some sauce to go along with it?

C : Some <u>chili sauce</u> and <u>soy sauce</u> would be great.

S : Anything to drink?

C : Can I have a <u>hot milk tea</u>, please?

S : Anything else?

C : No, that'll be all. Thanks.

S : Would you like any cutlery?

C : <u>A pair of chopsticks</u> and <u>a straw</u>, please.

S : Sure. You total will be <u>sixty-five</u> dollars, please.

C : Here you are.

Taiwanese Breakfast Menu

			Drinks	
Clay oven roll (with or without egg) 燒餅（夾蛋／不要夾蛋）		$40		
Flaky scallion pancake 蔥抓餅		$50	Hot / Cold Soybean Milk 熱／冰 豆漿	$30
Pork bun 肉包		$20	Rice & Peanut milk 米漿	$20
Vegetable bun 菜包		$20		
Turnip cake / Radish cake (with thick soy sauce / with chili sauce) 蘿蔔糕（加醬油膏／加辣椒）		$35	Hot / Cold Milk Tea 熱／冰 奶茶	$20
Steamed pork buns in a bamboo steamer (10 pieces) 一龍小籠湯包 10 粒）		$80		
Scallion pancake 蔥油餅		$50		
Steamed bun (with or without egg) 饅頭（夾蛋／不要夾蛋）		$35		
Taiwanese sweet glutinous rice roll 紫米飯糰		$40		
Taiwanese glutinous rice roll 飯糰		$40		
Taiwanese omelet 蛋餅		$30		
Thin green onion cake with twisted cruller 煎餅油條		$30		
Twisted cruller / Fried bread stick 油條		$35		
Salted soymilk 鹹豆漿		$40		

Unit 4

Pizza
披薩

Learning Objectives

What you will learn in this unit…

• How to serve pizza.
• How to order pizza.
• Different types of pizza toppings and crusts.
• Keyword verbs, phrases and idioms used when serving or ordering pizza.

Brainstorming

What does your favorite pizza topping say about you?

☐ Cheese / 起士

☐ Ham / 火腿

☐ Pineapple / 鳳梨

☐ Pepperoni / 美式臘腸

☐ Sausage / 香腸

· ·

1. What toppings do you like on your pizza?
   (Examples: cheese, bacon, pepperoni, etc.)
2. What kind of pizza crust do you like?
   (Examples: thin & crispy, pan pizza, etc.)
3. What is your favorite pizza restaurant?
   (Examples: Pizza Hut, Domino's, etc.)
4. Ask your partner what his/her favorite pizza toppings and crust are.

Pizza Topping　披薩配料

mushroom
蘑菇

onions
洋蔥

olives(green / black)
綠橄欖／黑橄欖

jalapeno
辣青椒

feta cheese
希臘羊奶起士

tomatoes
番茄

salmon
鮭魚

pepperoni
美式臘腸

red bell pepper /
green bell pepper /
yellow bell pepper
紅椒／青椒／黃椒

Pizza Size　披薩大小

a slice of pizza 一片披薩

personal pan pizza (P) 個人披薩

small (S) 小

medium (M) 中

large (L) 大

extra large / jumbo (XL) 無敵大／特大

delivery
外送

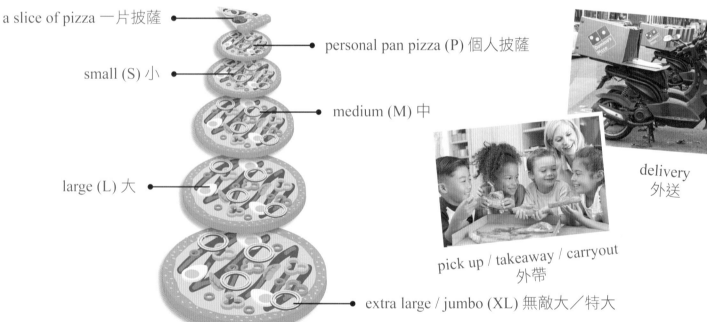

pick up / takeaway / carryout
外帶

Pizza Crusts　披薩種類

thin and crispy
薄皮餅皮

stuffed (cheesy) crust
芝心餅皮

classic
經典餅皮

pan pizza
厚皮餅皮

PREVIEW & IN CLASS PRACTICE

Practice Phrases

Work with a partner to practice saying the phrases below.

Making Offers – Server	Making Requests – Customer
How can I help you?	I'd like to order some pizzas.
Will that be delivery or pickup?	Delivery. Pickup.
Can I have your phone number?	It's 0987-123-456.
Is your address number 1, Da-An Road, Section 2?	Yes, that's correct. No. I'm afraid not. It's number 2, Ren-Ai Road, Section 2.
What would you like to order today?	I'd like a medium pepperoni pizza, please. I'd like a large Hawaiian pizza, please. I'd like two extra large ham and sausage pizzas, please. I'd like three jumbo Super Supreme pizzas, please.
What kind of crust would you like?	Thin and crispy, please. Classic, please. Pan, please. Stuffed, please. Hand-tossed, please.
Do you have any coupons you'd like to use?	Yes, I do. No, I don't.

Listening Practice

 track 15

Listen to the audio. Listen to what the server and customer want, and then choose the correct answer.

1. ○ (A) The customer is a Hawaiian.

   ○ (B) The customer wants to order two Hawaiian pizzas.

2. ○ (A) The customer wants to order three jumbo size pepper pizzas.

   ○ (B) The customer wants to order three jumbo size pepperoni pizzas.

3. ○ (A) The customer wants a thin and crispy crust.

   ○ (B) The customer is thin and crispy.

4. ○ (A) The customer can pick up his pizza in 30 minutes.

   ○ (B) The delivery man will deliver the pizza in 30 minutes.

CONVERSATION

 Track 16

*It is Friday night. Ken is inviting some friends over to his place to watch a football game. He decided to order some pizzas over the phone from Pizza House for his **buddies**[1].*

H : Host   K : Ken

H : Pizza House. How can I help you?

K : Hi! I'd like to order some pizzas, please.

H : [a] <u>Will that be **delivery**[2] or **pickup**[3]?</u>

K : Delivery, please.

H : Can I have your phone number, please?

K : It's 2879-2098.

H : Mr. Ken Chang?

K : Yes, that's right.

H : Is your address Number 2, High Street?

K : That's correct.

H : What would you like to order today?

K : [b] <u>I'd like one **jumbo**[4] **pepperoni**[5],</u> one jumbo **Hawaiian**[6], one jumbo cheese and one jumbo **sausage**[7], <u>please.</u>

H : [c] <u>What kind of **crust**[8] would you like?</u>

K : I'd like **thin and crispy**[9] for the pepperoni and Hawaiian pizzas, and **stuffed crust**[10] for the cheese and sausage pizzas, please.

H : Is there anything else?

K : Yes. Can I have five large bottles of Coke, please?

H : [d] <u>We have a **special**[11] for today.</u> You get a free bottle of Coke with every order of a jumbo-sized pizza. Would you like that, sir?

K : That sounds wonderful. Is it for the same price though?

H : Yes, it is!

K : That sounds great! I'll have the special, please.

 New Words & Phrases Track 17 ─────

1. **buddy** (buddies, plural) (n.) 好友 / 密友
   反 enemy
   同 good friend
2. **delivery** (n.) 外送
3. **pickup** (n.) 外帶
   反 delivery
   同 carryout/takeaway/takeout
4. **jumbo** (n.) 無敵大 / 特大
   反 extra small
   同 extra large

5. **pepperoni** (n.) 美式臘腸
6. **Hawaiian** (adj.) 夏威夷的
7. **sausage** (n.) 香腸
8. **crust** (n.) 餅皮
9. **thin and crispy** (phrase) 薄脆餅皮
10. **stuffed** (cheesy) **crust** (phrase) 芝心餅皮
11. **special** (adj.) 特價

H : ^e <u>Your pizza will be there within thirty minutes.</u> The total is $97.80.

　　 ^f <u>Are there any **coupons**[12] you'd like to use today?</u>

K : But, can I still use the coupon with the special for today?

H : Yes, you can.

K : That sounds great!

H : What kind of coupon do you have?

K : I have a "**buy one get one free**" [13] coupon.

H : Do you have the **promotion code**[14], sir?

K : Let me see... It's GC239871.

H : Okay. After the **discount**[15], your total is $56.40.

K : Thank you.

H : Have a nice day, sir.

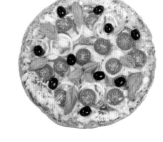

Q & A

1. Why did Ken want to order pizzas?

　　_____

2. What is Ken's street address?

　　_____

3. What sizes and pizzas did Ken order?

　　_____

4. What kind of crust did Ken want for his pepperoni and Hawaiian pizzas?

　　_____

5. How much were the pizzas and Coke before using the coupon?

　　_____

Important!

Speaking Practice Exercise

a. Will that be delivery or pickup?
外送或外帶呢？

b. I'd like one jumbo pepperoni pizza, please.
請給我一個特大美式臘腸披薩。

c. What kind of crust would you like?
你要用什麼餅皮呢？

d. We have a special for today.
我們今日有個特價。

e. Your pizza will be there within thirty minutes.
你的披薩 30 分鐘內到。

f. Are there any coupons you'd like to use today?
你今天要使用優惠券嗎？

---

12. **coupon** (n.) 優惠券

13. **buy one get one free** (phrase) 買一送一

14. **promotion code** (n.) 優惠券代號 / 代碼

15. **discount** (tr. v./n.) 折扣

Vocabulary Review

Antonym

1. delivery: _____
2. buddy: _____
3. jumbo: _____
4. small: _____

Synonym

1. buddy: _____
2. jumbo: _____
3. pickup: _____
4. discount: _____

Match the Chinese-English Translations

1.(　) Delivery	a.	薄脆餅皮
2.(　) Pickup	b.	芝心餅皮
3.(　) Jumbo	c.	一片披薩
4.(　) Pepperoni	d.	個人披薩
5.(　) Crust	e.	厚皮披薩
6.(　) Thin and crispy	f.	外帶
7.(　) Stuffed (cheesy) crust	g.	無敵大 / 特大
8.(　) A slice of pizza	h.	美式臘腸
9.(　) Personal pan pizza	i.	餅皮
10.(　) Pan pizza	j.	外送

Track 18

Listen and Pronounce

Listen to the audio first. Then, try pronouncing each one of the pizza toppings below.

• Black olives 黑橄欖	• Calamari 花枝	• Feta cheese 希臘羊奶起士	• Fresh asparagus 蘆筍
• Fresh tomato 蕃茄	• Green peppers 青椒	• Grilled chicken 烤雞胸肉	• Ham 火腿
• Italian sausage 義大利香腸	• Jalapeno 辣青椒	• Mozzarella cheese 莫札瑞拉起士	• Mushrooms 蘑菇
• Pepperoni 美式臘腸	• Pineapple 鳳梨	• Red bell pepper 紅椒	• Salami 沙拉米
• Sausage 香腸	• Shrimp 蝦仁	• Smoked salmon 煙燻鮭魚	• Spinach 菠菜

Exercise

Draw a pizza from the smallest to the largest, then name their individual sizes.

Draw	▲				
Name the size	Example: A slice of pizza				

Make your own pizza

Example

"I'd like to have one <u>medium</u> <u>Italian sausage</u> and <u>pepperoni</u> pizza."

(I)   (II)   (III)

Now, try to fill in the blanks below using the following choices.

I. Sizes of pizza

Small (S), Medium (M), Large (L), Extra Large/Jumbo (XL)

II. Pizza toppings: Choose two toppings from the below choices.

a. Black olives 黑橄欖	b. Calamari 花枝	c. Feta cheese 希臘羊奶起士	d. Fresh asparagus 蘆筍
e. Fresh tomato 蕃茄	f. Green peppers 青椒	g. Grilled chicken 烤雞胸肉	h. Ham 火腿
i. Italian sausage 義大利香腸	j. Jalapeno 辣青椒	k. Mozzarella cheese 莫札瑞拉起士	l. Mushrooms 蘑菇
m. Pepperoni 美式臘腸	n. Pineapple 鳳梨	o. Red bell pepper 紅椒	p. Salami 沙拉米
q. Sausage 香腸	r. Shrimp 蝦仁	s. Smoked salmon 煙燻鮭魚	t. Spinach 菠菜

1. I'd like to have one _____ _____ and _____ pizza.

                    (I) size   (II) topping   (III) topping

2. I'd like to have one _____ _____ and _____ pizza.

                    (I) size   (II) topping   (III) topping

3. I'd like to have one _____ _____ and _____ pizza.

                    (I) size   (II) topping   (III) topping

4. I'd like to have one _____ _____ and _____ pizza.

                    (I) size   (II) topping   (III) topping

5. I'd like to have one _____ _____ and _____ pizza.

                    (I) size   (II) topping   (III) topping

Photographs

Choose the sentence that best describes the below pictures.

1. (A) The man is ordering pizza over the phone.
   (B) The man is taking a pizza order over the phone.
   (C) The man is delivering a pizza.
   (D) The man is picking up a pizza.

   Your answer: (   )

2. (A) It looks like a customer making her own pizza.
   (B) It looks like a customer choosing her own pizza toppings.
   (C) It looks like a man is delivering pizzas.
   (D) It looks like a man is picking up pizzas.

   Your answer: (   )

In-Class Role Play

Firstly, place the below sentences in the correct order. Then, using your answers, practice the conversation. One student plays the role of server, and the other, the customer. Using the below menu, try to order different types of items. Replace the underlined words with different items on the menu. Practice as many times as possible, ordering different items from the menu, and changing roles.

(   ) a.   <u>Delivery</u>, please.

(   ) b.   Can I have your phone number, please?

(   ) c.   It's <u>0912-345-678</u>.

(   ) d.   <u>Mr. Henry Lee</u>? Is your address <u>Number 22, Jien-Guo Road</u>?

(   ) e.   That's correct.

(   ) f.   What would you like to order today?

(   ) g.   No, that's it.

(   ) h.   Your pizza will be there within thirty minutes. The total is <u>$8.80</u>.

(   ) i.   Ok. Thank you.

(   ) j.   Have a nice day, sir.

(   ) k.   I'd like <u>one medium Chicken Lover's</u> pizza, please.

(   ) l.   What kind of crust would you like?

(   ) m.   I'd like a <u>classic</u> crust, please.

(   ) n.   Is there anything else?

(   ) o.   <u>New York</u> Pizza. How can I help you?

(   ) p.   I'd like to order some pizzas, please.

(   ) q.   Will that be delivery or pickup?

Personal pan	(3 inches)	$3.95
Small	(6 inches)	$8.95
Medium	(9 inches)	$14.95
Large	(12 inches)	$16.95

CHOOSE YOUR CRUST

Thin 'n Crispy

Stuffed Crust

Classic

Pan Pizza

CHOOSE YOUR OWN TOPPING
Personal $1.50 Small $2.00 Medium $2.50 Large $3.00

Olive
Button mushroom
Calamari
Feta cheese
Asparagus
Tomato
Green pepper
Grilled chicken
Ham
Italian sausage

Mozzarella cheese
Mushroom
Pepperoni
Pineapple
Red bell pepper
Salami
Sausage
Shrimp
Smoked salmon
Spinach

Pizzas

Cheese

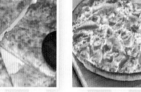
Ham

BBQ Chicken

Hawaiian

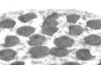
Pepperoni

Sausage

Veggie Lover's

Supreme

Unit 5

Learning Objectives

What you will learn in this unit⋯
- How to order at a drive-thru'?
- How to take an order at a drive-thru'?
- How to reply to a request for the use of mobile payments?
- Learn how to choose and order your toppings for hotdogs, burgers and sandwiches.

Brainstorming

Can you name some famous drive-thru' fast food restaurants?

☐ In-N-Out drive-thru'In-N-Out
得來速

☐ Taco Bell drive-thru'
塔可鐘得來速

☐ Wendy's drive-thru'
溫蒂得來速

☐ Arby's drive thru' 阿比得來速

☐ A&W drive thru'A&W 得來速

. . . .

1. Can you name some other drive-thru' fast food restaurants? (Example: KFC (Kentucky Fried Chicken).)
2. Can you name some toppings on a hotdog, burger or sandwich? (Example: BBQ sauce.)
3. Can you name some milkshake flavors? (Example: Strawberry milkshake.)
4. Can you name some mix-ins for milkshakes? (Example: Oreo cookies.)
5. Ask your partner what kinds of toppings he/she likes on his/her burger, hotdog or sandwich?

KEY WORDS

road trip to the countryside
開車旅行到鄉村

Five Guys drive-thru'
五兄弟得來速

Kosher style hotdog
猶太風格熱狗

Cajun style fries
凱真風味薯條

speaking directly into a microphone
直接對著麥克風講話

milkshake mix-ins
奶昔配料

bacon and cherry milkshake
培根櫻桃奶昔

pay using Apple Pay
透過蘋果行動支付

reader
讀卡機

Apple Pay 蘋果行動支付／
Mobile payment 行動支付

PREVIEW & IN CLASS PRACTICE

Practice Phrases

Work with a partner to practice saying the phrases below between an order-taker and a customer.

Order-taker	Customer
Welcome to Five Guys. May I take your order?	I would like to have a Kosher Style hotdog, a cheeseburger, one large fries and a coffee milkshake, please.
I'm sorry, sir. Can you speak directly into the microphone? I can barely hear you.	Oh, okay. I would like to have a Kosher Style hotdog, a cheeseburger, one large fries and a coffee milkshake, please.
Would you like our Five Guys Style fries or Cajun Style fries?	Five Guys Style fries, please.
What kind of toppings would you like for your cheeseburger?	How many toppings can I choose?
You can choose as many as you like.	Oh, okay. I'll have the lettuce, relish and A1 sauce, please.
Sure. Would you like any other mix-ins for your milkshake?	How many mix-ins can I have?
You can have as many mix-ins as you like.	Ok. Can I add the bacon, salted caramel and cherries, please?
Sure. So that's one Kosher Style hotdog, one cheeseburger with lettuce, relish and A1 sauce; one large Five Guys Style fries; and one coffee, bacon, salted caramel and cherries milkshake.	That's right!
Would you like anything else?	No, that'll be all.

Listening Practice Track 19

Listen to the audio. Listen to the conversation between the order-taker/server and the customer, and then choose the correct answer.

1. ○ (A) There are five guys ordering hotdogs and milkshakes.

   ○ (B) A customer is ordering a hotdog and a milkshake at Five Guys Burger & Fries.

2. ○ (A) The customer would like to order a Cajun Style hotdog and a strawberry milkshake.

   ○ (B) The customer would like to order a Kosher Style hotdog and a strawberry milkshake.

3. ○ (A) The customer ordered a large Five Guys Style fries.

   ○ (B) The customer ordered a large Cajun Style fries.

4. ○ (A) The customer ordered a cheeseburger with lettuce, relish and A1 sauce.

   ○ (B) The customer ordered a large cheeseburger with lettuce, relish and A1 sauce.

5. ○ (A) The customer ordered a strawberry, salted caramel and cherries milkshake.

   ○ (B) The customer ordered a strawberry and cherries milkshake.

*Ken and Michelle are planning to go on a **road trip**[1] to the **countryside**[2]. They decided to go to a **drive-thru**[3] at **Five Guys Burger & Fries**[4] to get a quick lunch.*

O：**Order-taker**[5]   **K**：Ken   **C**：Cashier   **S**：Server

....

O : Welcome to Five Guys. May I take your order?

K : [a] I would like to have a **Kosher Style hotdog**[6], a **cheeseburger**[7], one large fries and a coffee **milkshake**[8], please.

O : I'm sorry, sir. [b] Can you **speak directly into the microphone**[9][10]? [c] I can **barely**[11] hear you.

K : Oh, okay. I would like to have a Kosher Style hotdog, a cheeseburger, one large fries and a coffee milkshake, please.

O : [d] Would you like our **Five Guys Style fries**[12] or **Cajun Style fries**[13]?

K : Five Guys Style fries, please.

O : [e] What kind of **toppings**[14] would you like for your cheeseburger?

K : [f] How many toppings can I choose?

O : [g] You can choose as many as you like.

K : Oh, okay. [h] I'll have the **lettuce**[15], **relish**[16] and **A1 sauce**[17], please.

New Words & Phrases

 Track 21

1. **road trip** (n.)　開車旅行
2. **countryside** (n.)　鄉村
   反 city
3. **drive-thru** (n.)　得來速
   反 eat-in / walk-in
4. **Five Guys Burger & Fries** (n.)
   五兄弟漢堡薯條
5. **order-taker** (n.)　訂單接受者
6. **Kosher Style hotdog** (n.)　猶太風格熱狗
7. **cheeseburger** (n.)　單層起司
   反 double cheeseburger
8. **milkshake** (n.)　奶昔
   同 shake(s)

9. **speak directly into the microphone** (phrase)
   直接對著麥克風講話
   同 ask directly　反 speak indirectly
10. **microphone** (n.)　麥克風
11. **barely** (ad.)　勉強
    同 hardly
12. **Five Guys Style fries** (n.)　五兄弟風味薯條
13. **Cajun Style fries** (n.)
    凱真 / 肯瓊 / 凱郡 / 卡津 風味薯條，
    Cajun 意指移居美國路易斯安納州的法人後裔
14. **toppings** (n.)　配料
    同 garnishes
15. **lettuce** (n.)　生菜 / 萵苣
16. **relish** (n.)　切細碎的酸黃瓜

O : Sure. [i] Would you like any other mix-ins for your milkshake?

K : How many mix-ins can I have?

O : [j] You can have as many **mix-ins**[18] as you like.

K : Ok. Can I add the **bacon**[19], **salted caramel**[20] and **cherries**[21], please?

O : Sure. So that's one Kosher Style hotdog, one cheeseburger with lettuce, relish and A1 sauce; one large Five Guys Style fries; and one coffee, bacon, salted caramel and cherries milkshake.

K : That's right!

O : Would you like anything else?

K : No, that'll be all.

O : [k] Please **drive up**[22] to the next window.

Ken drives up to the next window.

C : [l] That'll be $13.27 (thirteen, twenty-seven), please.

K : [m] Do you accept **Apple Pay**[23]?

C : **Yup!**[24] [n] Just a second... Here's the **reader**[25].

Ken holds his cellphone near the reader.

[Beep!][26]

S : Ok. You're done. [o] Just drive up to the next window to **pick up**[27] your order.

Ken drives up to the next window to pick up his order.

S : Here you go.

K : Thanks.

S : Have a nice day!

K : You too!

---

17. **A1 sauce** (n.)　A1 醬料

18. **mix-ins** (n.)　配料
    同 blend ins

19. **bacon** (n.)　培根

20. **salted caramel** (n.)　海鹽焦糖

21. **cherries** (n.)　櫻桃

22. **drive up** (ph.)　把車子往前開
    反 drive back

23. **Apple Pay** (n.)　蘋果行動支付
    同 mobile payment / mobile wallet
    反 cash payment

24. **Yup!**　是的
    同 Yes!
    反 Nope! / No!

25. **reader** (n.)　讀卡機

26. **Beep!** (n.)　嗶一聲

27. **pick up** (food) (v.)　去領取（餐點）
    同 collect
    反 delivery

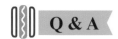

1. Where did Ken and Michelle get their lunch at?

   _____

2. What types of fries does Five Guys Burger & Fries offer?

   _____

3. What kind of toppings did Ken choose for his cheeseburger?

   _____

4. How many mix-ins can Ken choose for his milkshake?

   _____

5. How much was the cost of the meal?

   _____

Important!
Speaking Practice Exercise

Practice saying the below short sentences.

a. I would like to have a Kosher Style hotdog, a cheeseburger, one large fries and a coffee milkshake, please.
   請給我一個猶太教風味熱狗、一個單層起司堡、一份薯條還有一杯咖啡奶昔。

b. Can you speak directly into the microphone?
   你可以直接對著麥克風講話嗎？

c. I can barely hear you.
   我幾乎聽不見你的聲音。

d. Would you like our Five Guys Style fries or Cajun Style fries?
   您要點我們的五兄弟風味薯條還是凱真風味薯條呢？

e. What kind of toppings would you like for your cheeseburger?
   你的單層起司漢堡要加什　配料呢？

f. How many toppings can I choose?
   我可以選擇多少配料呢？

g. You can choose as many as you like.
   你可以隨心所欲加選你喜歡的配料。

h. I'll have the lettuce, relish and A1 sauce, please.
   請給我生菜、切碎的酸黃瓜以及 A1 醬。

i. Would you like any other mix-ins for your milkshake?
   您的奶昔要加其他配料嗎？

j. You can have as many mix-ins as you like.
   您可以隨心所欲加選配料．

k. Please drive up to the next window.
   請往前開到下一個窗口。

l. That'll be $13.27 (thirteen, twenty-seven), please.
   總共是十三塊二十七元。

m. Do you accept Apply Pay?
   你們接受 APPLE 行動支付嗎？

n. Just a second… Here's the reader.
   稍等一下…讀卡機在這。

o. Just drive up to the next window to pick up your order.
   請往前開到下一個窗口領取你的餐點。

What's in a burger?

Fill in the blanks using the words given below

a. cheese	b. patty
c. bacon	d. ketchup
e. bun	f. lettuce
g. pickles	h. tomatoes
i. patty	

Listen and Pronounce Track 22

Listen to the audio, and then try to pronounce each one of the following items:

HotdogS 熱狗

• Kosher Style Hotdog 猶太教風味熱狗	• Cheese Dog 起司熱狗	• Bacon Dog 培根熱狗
• Bacon Cheese 培根起司		

burgers 漢堡

• Hamburger 單層漢堡	• Cheeseburger 單層起司漢堡	• Bacon Burger 單層培根漢堡
• Bacon Cheeseburger 單層培根起司漢堡		

Sandwiches 三明治

• Veggie Sandwich 蔬菜三明治	• Cheese Veggie Sandwich 起司蔬菜三明治	• Grilled Cheese Sandwich 烤起司三明治

FRIES 薯條

• Five Guys Style Fries 五兄弟風味薯條	• Cajun Style Fries 凱真風味薯條

TOPPINGS 配料

• Green Peppers 青椒	• Mushrooms 蘑菇	• Hot sauce 辣醬
• Jalapeno 墨西哥辣椒	• Ketchup 番茄醬	• Lettuce 生菜
• Mayo (mayonnaise) 美乃滋	• Mustard 黃芥末	• Fresh Onions 洋蔥
• Grilled Onions 烤洋蔥	• Pickles 醃黃瓜	• Relish 切碎的酸黃瓜
• Tomatoes 番茄		

▌ Listen and fill in the blanks

Track 23

Listen to the conversation and fill in the blanks.

1. The customer ordered a bacon dog with _____ and _____ toppings.

2. The customer ordered one large _____ Style fries.

3. The customer ordered a _____ and banana milkshake.

4. The order-taker said that the customer can have as many ___-___ as he likes in his bacon milkshake.

5. The customer paid $8.50 using _____ Pay.

▌ Photographs

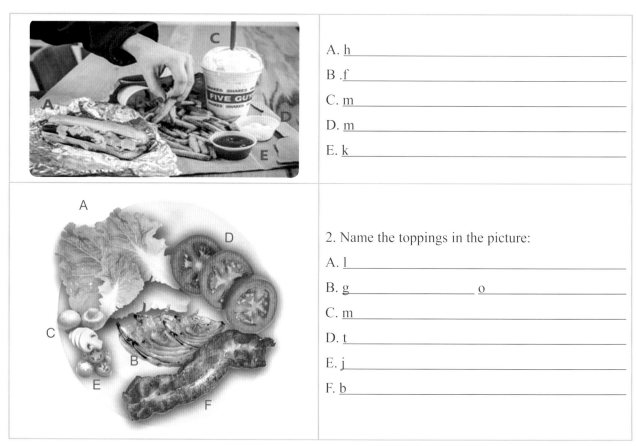

A. h _____

B. f _____

C. m _____

D. m _____

E. k _____

2. Name the toppings in the picture:

A. l _____

B. g _____ o _____

C. m _____

D. t _____

E. j _____

F. b _____

In-Class Role Play

Practice Role Play Exercise 1

- Using the below short conversation, ask each student to find a partner to practice with. One student plays the role of server (S), and the other, the customer (C).
- Then, change roles.

Practice Role Play Exercise 2

- Now, practice again. This time, using the below menu, ask the students to replace the underlined words with items from the menu.

SHORT CONVERSATION PRACTICE

C : Customer　客戶　　　S1, S2 : Server 1, Server 2　（服務生 1, 服務生 2）

S1 : Welcome to Five Guys. May I take your order?

C : I would like to have a Kosher Style hotdog, a cheeseburger and one large fries, please.

S1 : I'm sorry, sir. Can you speak directly into the microphone? I can barely hear you.

C : Oh, okay. I would like to have a Kosher Style hotdog, a cheeseburger, and one large fries, please.

S1 : What kind of toppings would you like for your cheeseburger?

C : I'll have the lettuce, relish and A1 sauce, please.

S1 : Would you like our Five Guys Style fries or Cajun Style fries?

C : Five Guys Style fries, please.

S1 : Sure. So that's one Kosher Style hotdog, one cheeseburger with lettuce, relish and A1 sauce; and one large Five Guys Style fries.

C : That's right!

S1 : Would you like anything else?

C : No, that'll be all.

S1 : Please drive up to the next window.

MENU
BURGERS, HOTDOGS & SANDWICHES

(a1) HOTDOGS 熱狗

Kosher Style Hotdog 猶太風格熱狗	$4.09
Cheese Dog 起司熱狗	$4.79
Bacon Dog 培根熱狗	$5.09
Bacon Cheese Dog 培根起司熱狗	$5.99

(a2) BURGERS 漢堡

Hamburger 漢堡	$6.09
Cheeseburger 起司漢堡	$6.99
Bacon Burger 培根漢堡	$7.09
Bacon Cheeseburger 培根起司漢堡	$7.99

(a3) SANDWICHES 三明治

Veggie Sandwich 蔬菜三明治	$3.29
Cheese Veggie Sandwich 起司蔬菜三明治	$3.99
Grilled Cheese Sandwich 烤起司三明治	$4.10
BLT 三明治	$5.99

培根、蔬菜、番茄三明治（Bacon, Lettuce, Tomato，簡稱 BLT 三明治）

TOPPINGS 配料
ALL TOPPINGS ARE FREE!

Choose as many as you like! 你可以隨心所欲加選你喜歡的配料！

What's in a burger?　圖解漢堡

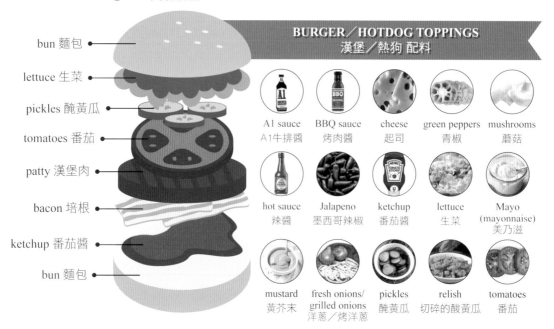

MILKSHAKE MIX-INS 奶昔配料
手工製香草奶昔可選擇是否要加入鮮奶油。

您可隨意選擇我們的多種免費配料：

Unit 6

Learning Objectives

What you will learn in this unit…

- How to serve coffee at a café.
- How to order coffee at a café.
- Different types of coffee.
- Keyword verbs, phrases and idioms used at a café.

Brainstorming

What is your favorite café, and what does it say about you?

☐ Cama Café
咖碼咖啡館

☐ Mr. Brown Cafe
伯朗咖啡館

☐ Starbucks
星巴克

☐ Louisa Coffee
路易莎咖啡

☐ Ikari Coffee
怡客咖啡

1. What is your favorite type of coffee?
   (Examples: latte, cappuccino, etc.)
2. How do you like your coffee?
   (Examples: black, with sugar, with cream only, etc.)
3. Ask your partner what is his/her favorite café and type of coffee.

KEY WORDS

Coffee Size　飲料大小

-NOTE-
short = small 小杯
tall = medium 中杯
grande = large 大杯
venti = extra large 特大杯

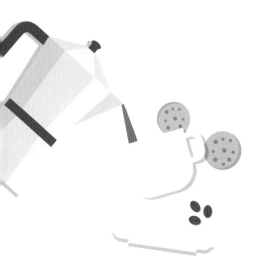

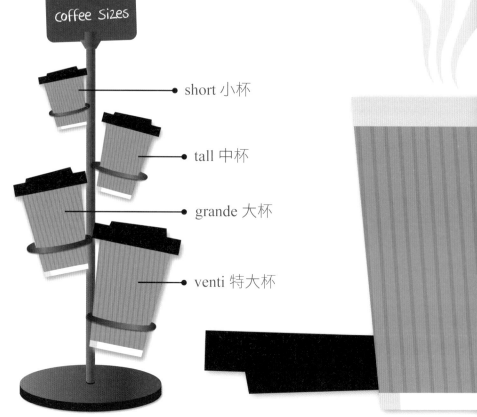

coffee sizes

- short 小杯
- tall 中杯
- grande 大杯
- venti 特大杯

Type of Coffee Drinks　咖啡飲品

Latte
拿鐵

Cappuccino
卡布奇諾

Chocolate Mocha
摩卡咖啡

Caramel macchiato
焦糖瑪奇朵

Irish Coffee
愛爾蘭咖啡

Espresso
濃縮咖啡

Americano
美式黑咖啡

Frappuccino
星冰樂

French Vanilla
Hazelnut Latte
法式香草榛果拿鐵

Hazelnut Latte
榛果拿鐵

PREVIEW & IN CLASS PRACTICE

Practice Phrases

Work with a partner to practice saying the phrases below.

Making Offers – Server	Making Requests – Customer
What can I get for you today?	I'd like to have a cappuccino, please. I'd like to have a latte, please. I'd like an espresso, please. I'd like to have a mocha, please. I'd like to have a caramel macchiato, please. I'd like to have a frappuccino, please.
What size would you like?	Small (short), please. Medium (tall), please. Large (grande), please. Extra large (venti), please.
How would you like your coffee?	Just two creams, please. Just two sugars, please. Two creams and two sugars, please. One cream and one sugar, please. Just one cream, please.

Track 24

Listening Practice

Listen to the audio. Listen to the conversation between the hostess and customer, and then choose the correct answer.

1. ○ (A) The customer ordered a small latte, to go.

   ○ (B) The customer ordered a small latte, for here.

2. ○ (A) The customer ordered a small black coffee and a large cappuccino.

   ○ (B) The customer ordered a small cappuccino and a large black coffee.

3. ○ (A) The customer ordered two large black coffee with one cream.

   ○ (B) The customer ordered a large black coffee with two creams.

4. ○ (A) The customer thinks that the server is tall and expressive.

   ○ (B) The customer wants to have a tall espresso.

CONVERSATION

 Track 25

*Michelle and Penny were feeling very **exhausted**[1] after a long **luncheon meeting**[2] at work. Both of them decided to go to Starlight **Café**[3] to **lighten up**[4].*

C : Cashier   **M** : Michelle   **P** : Penny   **B** : Barista

C : Hi! How are you doing today?

M : Great! How are you?

C : Great! Thank you. [a] What can I get for you today?

M : I'd like to have a **coffee**[5], please.

C : [b] What size would you like? [c] We have four sizes: **short**[6], **tall**[7], **grande**[8] and **venti**[9].

M : Tall, please.

C : [d] How would you like your coffee?

M : [e] Two **creams**[10] and two sugars, please.

C : Sure. And, what's your name?

M : It's Michelle.

C : For here or to go?

M : For here, please.

C : OK. One tall, black coffee, for here. That'll be $1.75, please.

M : Here you go.

C : Three twenty-five ($3.25) is your **change**[11]. Have a nice day, ma'am.

M : You too.

It was Penny's turn to order coffee now.

C : Hi! How are you doing today?

P : Great! How are you?

C : Great! Thank you. What can I get for you today?

P : I'll have a grande **caramel macchiato**[12], please.

C : What's your name?

 New Words & Phrases Track 26

1. **exhausted** (v.)　筋疲力盡 / 累翻了
   反 energy
2. **luncheon meeting** (n.)　午宴 / 正式的午餐
3. **café** (n.)　咖啡館
   同 Coffee house/coffee bar
4. **lighten up** (v.)　放輕鬆
5. **coffee** (n.)　咖啡
   同 caffè
6. **short** (as in size)
   小杯（星巴克專用飲料杯大小名稱）
   反 grande
7. **tall** (as in size) (adj.)
   中杯（星巴克專用飲料杯大小名稱）
   同 medium
8. **grande** (as in size) (adj.)
   大杯（星巴克專用飲料杯大小名稱）
   反 short/small　同 large
9. **venti** (as in size) (adj.)
   特大杯（星巴克專用飲料杯大小名稱）
   同 extra large
10. **cream** (n.)　奶精 / 奶球
    同 creamer
11. **change** (n.)　找錢 / 零錢
    反 notes　同 coins
12. **caramel macchiato** (n.)　焦糖瑪奇朵

P : It's Penny.

C : For here or to go?

P : For here, please.

C : OK. That'll be $1.95, please.

P : Here you go.

C : Here's a **nickel**[13] ($0.05). Have a nice day, ma'am.

P : You too.

*A few minutes later, the **barista**[14] **hailed**[15] out.*

B : Michelle⋯A tall coffee with two creams and two sugars, for here!

M : Thank you.

B : Penny⋯A grande, caramel macchiato, for here.

M : Thank you.

*Michelle and Penny **picked up**[16] their coffee at the counter and found a place by the window.*

Q & A

1. What did Michelle order?

2. What coffee sizes does Starlight Café offer?

3. How much is Michelle's change?

4. What did Penny order?

5. How much is Penny's change?

Important!
Speaking Practice Exercise

a. What can I get for you today?
請問你今天想點什麼呢？

b. What size would you like?
你要什麼大小呢？

c. We have four sizes: short, tall, grande and venti.
我們有四種大小：小、中、大及特大。

d. How would you like your coffee?
你咖啡要怎麼喝？

e. Two creams and two sugars, please.
請加兩份奶精和兩份糖。

13. **nickel** (n.) 五分（$0.05）
    同 five cents
14. **barista** (n.) 咖啡師傅（門市中調理咖啡的人）
15. **hail** (v.) 招呼
16. **picked up** (v.) 拾起／撿起來

Vocabulary Review

Antonym	Synonym
1. exhausted: _____	1. tall (size): _____
2. for here: _____	2. grande (size): _____
3. change: _____	3. venti (size): _____
4. short (size) _____	4. café: _____

What can I get for you today?

Fill in the blanks with different (a) sizes, and (b) types of coffee as shown below:

Example

    I'd like   <u>a/two</u>   <u>small</u>   <u>Frappuccino</u>, please.

               (how many)   (a) size   (b) coffee

(a) Sizes: small, medium, large, extra large

    Starbucks sizes: short, tall, grande and venti

(b) Types of coffee drinks:

    1. Americano   美式咖啡 / 黑咖啡

    2. Cappuccino   卡布奇諾

    3. Caramel Macchiato   焦糖瑪奇朵

    4. Chocolate Mocha   摩卡咖啡

    5. Espresso   濃縮咖啡

    6. Frappuccino   星冰樂

    7. Hazelnut Latte   榛果拿鐵

    8. Honey Latte   蜂蜜拿鐵

    9. Salted Caramel Latte   海鹽焦糖拿鐵

    10. Vanilla Latte   香草拿鐵

Exercise

1. I'd like _____ _____ _____ , please.

        (how many)   (a) size   (b) coffee

2. I'd like _____ _____ _____ , please.

         (a) size   (b) coffee

3. I'd like _____ _____ _____ , please.

         (b) coffee

4. I'd like _____ _____ _____ , please.

        (how many)   (a) size   (b) coffee

5. I'd like _____ _____ _____ , please.

        (how many)   (a) size   (b) coffee

How do you like your coffee?

Match the pictures to the answers given below.

a. One shot espresso	b. Coffee with foam	c. Coffee with three sugars
d. Iced black coffee	e. Iced milk coffee	f. Black coffee
g. Coffee with fresh milk	h. Two shots of espresso	

1. _____

2. _____

3. _____

4. _____

5. _____

6. _____

7. _____

8. _____

Track 27

Listen and Pronouncee

Listen to the audio first. Then, try pronouncing each one of the coffees on the menu below.

• Americano 美式咖啡	• Mocha 摩卡
• Cappuccino 卡布奇諾	• Caramel java chip frappuccino blended beverage 焦糖可可碎片星冰樂
• Caramel macchiato 焦糖瑪奇朵	• Coffee frappuccino blended beverage 咖啡星冰樂
• Dark mocha frappuccino blended beverage 黑摩卡可可碎片星冰樂	• Espresso frappuccino blended beverage 濃縮星冰樂
• Espresso 濃縮咖啡	• Frappuccino 星冰樂

Photographs

Choose the answer that best describes the pictures.

1. What do you see in the picture?
   (A) A customer is ordering coffee.
   (B) A customer is paying for his coffee.
   (C) A barista is making coffee.
   (D) A barista is calling out a customer's name.

   Answer: (   )

2. What do you see in the picture?
   (A) A customer is asking about coffee sizes.
   (B) A customer is ordering coffee.
   (C) A customer is talking to a barista.
   (D) A customer is asking for some cream and sugar.

   Answer: (   )

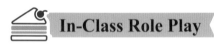

3. Write down the coffee sizes (a) to (d) on in the blanks given below.
   (A) _____
   (B) _____
   (C) _____
   (D) _____

In-Class Role Play

Firstly, place the below sentences in the correct order. Then, using your answers, practice the conversation. One student plays the role of server, and the other, the customer. Using the below menu, try to order different types of coffee. Replace the underlined words with different items on the menu. Practice as many times as possible, ordering different items from each menu above, and changing roles.

(   ) a. How would you like your coffee?

(   ) b. Just two sugars, please.

(   ) c. For here, please.

(   ) d. Ok. So that's one large, black coffee with two sugars, for here. That'll be $2.05, please.

(   ) e. Here you go.

(   ) f. Hi! What can I get for you today?

(   ) g. I'd like to have one black coffee, please.

(   ) h. What size would you like?

(   ) i. I'd like a large size, please.

(   ) j. For here or to go?

(   ) k. Ninety-five cents ($0.95) is your change. Have a nice day!

(   ) l. You too.

CLASSIC FAVORITES	TALL	GRANDE	VENTI
CAFFEE LATTE	$2.70	$3.25	$3.55
CAPPUCCINO	$2.70	$3.25	$3.55
CARAMEL MACCHIATO	$3.15	$3.70	$4.00
CAFFEE MOCHA	$3.00	$3.55	$9.85
WHITE CHOCOLATE MOCHA	$3.40	$3.95	$4.40
CAFFEE AMERICANO	$1.95	$2.25	$2.50
VANILLA LATTE	$3.00	$3.55	$3.85
CINNAMON DOLCE LATTE	$3.40	$3.95	$4.40

	one shot	two shots
ESPRESSO	$1.55	$1.85
ESPRESSO MACCHIATO	$1.60	$1.95

Unit 7

Taiwanese Bubble Tea
台灣珍珠奶茶

Learning Objectives

What you will learn in this unit…

- How to serve bubble tea.
- How to order bubble tea.
- Names of famous bubble tea stores in Taiwan.
- How sweet do you like your bubble tea?
- Names of different types of bubble tea.
- How much ice would you like in your bubble tea?
- How hot would you like your bubble tea?
- Names of different types of bubble tea toppings/add-ons.
- Keywords, verbs, phrases and idioms used in serving & ordering bubble tea.

Brainstorming

What kind of bubble tea you like says about you?

☐ Milk tea / 奶茶

☐ Red bean milk tea
紅豆奶茶

☐ Black Boba milk tea
波霸奶茶

☐ White Boba milk tea
白珍珠奶茶

☐ Milk tea with lots of toppings
奶茶三兄弟（仙草＋布丁＋珍珠）

1. What is your favorite type of tea? (Example: Green tea, Oolong tea.)
2. What is your favorite drink at the bubble tea store? (Example: Taro milk tea)
3. How sweet do you like your bubble tea? (Example: Half sugar.)

What's in a cup of bubble tea? 分解珍珠奶茶

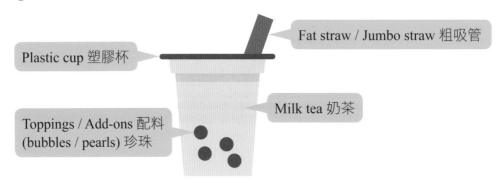

Fat straw / Jumbo straw 粗吸管

Plastic cup 塑膠杯

Milk tea 奶茶

Toppings / Add-ons 配料
(bubbles / pearls) 珍珠

Hot / Cold 熱 / 冷

Regular ice 正常冰	Less ice 少冰	Half ice 半冰	A little ice 微冰	Cold, but without ice 去冰	Room temperature 常溫	Hot 熱的

Sweetness Level 甜度

100% Regular Sugar 正常糖	70% Less Sugar 七分 / 少糖	50% Half Sugar 五分 / 半糖	30% One-third sugar / A little sugar 三分 / 微糖	0% Sugar-free 無糖

What kind of toppings would you like? 你想要加什麼料嗎？

Black Boba / black bubbles 黑波霸 / 黑珍珠	White Boba / White bubbles 白波霸 / 白珍珠	Red beans 紅豆	Green beans / Mung beans 綠豆	Grass jelly 仙草

Longan 桂圓	Coconut jelly 椰果	Pudding 布丁	Plum 梅子	Sweet potato balls 地瓜圓 Taro balls 芋圓

PREVIEW & IN CLASS PRACTICE

Practice Phrases

Work with a partner saying the following phrases between a customer and an order-taker at a Bubble Tea store.

Order-taker	Customer
Welcome to Boba Tea Café.	Can you recommend some of your customer's favorites?
Some of our customer's favorites are the taro bubble milk tea, matcha milk tea, coconut jelly bubble tea, black Boba milk tea, and white Boba milk tea.	• I'd like a white Boba milk tea, please. • One Boba milk tea, please.
What size would you like?	• I'd like a large, please. • Large, please. • I'd like a medium size, please. • Medium, please.
Would you like it hot/cold?	• Cold, please. • Hot, please.
If your customer says "cold", then ask, How much ice would you like? Regular ice, less ice, half ice, a little ice, or cold, but without ice?	• Regular ice, please. • Less ice, please. • Half ice, please. • A little ice, please. • Cold, but without ice, please.
If your customer says "hot", then ask, How hot would you like your drink?	• Room temperature, please. • Warm, please. • Hot, please.
We'll mix your drink with ice and then shake it using a cocktail mixer. The ice melts into the drink, and we'll drain the drink and leave the ice out so that it'll still be icy-cold.	What's cold, but without ice? • Wow! That sounds really cool. • I'll try that!
How much sugar would you like? There's regular sugar, less sugar, half sugar, a little sugar and sugar-free.	• Regular sugar, please. • Less sugar, please. • Half sugar, please. • A little sugar, please. • Sugar-free, please.

Listening Practice   Track 28

Listen to the audio. Listen to the conversation between a customer and a cashier at a Boba Tea Café, and then choose the correct answer.

1. ○ (A) The customer ordered a taro bubble milk tea.

   ○ (B) The customer ordered a matcha milk tea.

2. ○ (A) The customer ordered one large, half ice, light sugar, white Boba milk tea.

   ○ (B) The customer ordered one large, half ice, half sugar, white Boba milk tea.

3. ○ (A) The customer ordered one medium, hot, white Boba milk tea, sugar-free.

   ○ (B) The customer ordered one medium, hot, black Boba milk tea, sugar-free.

4. ○ (A) The customer handed the cashier $140.

   ○ (B) The customer handed the cashier $200.

5. ○ (A) The customer bought a bag for an extra two dollars and wanted his drinks placed together.

   ○ (B) The customer bought a bag for an extra two dollars and wanted his drinks placed separately.

CONVERSATION

Track 29

*Ken and Michelle are on a **walking tour**[1] under the **scorching summer heat**[2] in Taipei city. They decided to stop by at the **Boba Tea Café**[3].*

C：Cashier　**M**：Michelle　**K**：Ken

- -

C：Welcome to Boba Tea Café.

M：[a] <u>Can you recommend some of your customer's favorites?</u>

C：Some of our customer's favorites are the **taro bubble milk tea**[4], **matcha milk tea**[5], **coconut jelly bubble tea**[6], **black Boba milk tea**[7] and **white Boba milk tea**[8].

M：I'd like a white Boba milk tea, please.

C：[b] <u>What size would you like?</u>

M：I'd like a large, please.

C：[c] <u>Would you like it hot or cold?</u>

M：Cold, please.

C：[d] <u>How much ice would you like?</u> We have **regular ice**[9], **less ice**[10], **half ice**[11], **a little ice**[12], or **cold, but without ice**[13]?

M：[e] <u>What's cold, but without ice?</u>

C：We'll mix your drink with ice and then shake it using a **cocktail mixer**[14].The ice melts into the drink, and we'll **drain**[15] the drink and leave the ice out so that it'll still be **icy-cold**[16].

M：Wow! That sounds really cool. I'll try that!

C：[f] <u>How much sugar would you like?</u>

M：You can even choose how much sugar you want too?!

C：Yes! The Taiwanese are very **particular**[17] about their **sugar level**[18] **intake**[19]. There's **regular sugar**[20], **less sugar**[21], **half sugar**[22], **a little sugar**[23] and **sugar-free**[24].

M：Hmmm… **I'm on a diet**[25].

C：[g] <u>What about sugar-free?</u>

M：Sounds good to me!

The cashier then turned to Ken.

- -

C：What would you like to have?

K：[h] <u>I'll have the same.</u>

New Words & Phrases

Track 30

1. **walking tour** (n.)　徒步旅行
   - 同 sightseeing
   - 反 running tour

2. **scorching summer heat** (phrase)　火辣辣的夏天太陽
   - 同 burning summer heat
   - 反 freezing winter

3. **Boba Tea Café** (n.)　珍珠奶茶店
   （Boba 就是波霸的直譯 - 美國標準用法）

4. **taro bubble milk tea** (n.)　芋頭珍珠奶茶

5. **matcha milk tea** (n.)　抹茶奶茶

6. **coconut jelly bubble tea** (n.)　椰果奶茶

7. **black Boba milk tea** (n.)　黑波霸奶茶
   - 反 white Boba milk tea

8. **white Boba milk tea** (n.)　白波霸奶茶

9. **regular ice** (phrase)　正常冰
   - 同 with ice

10. **less ice** (phrase)　少冰

11. **half ice** (phrase)　半冰

12. **a little ice** (phrase)　微冰

13. **cold, but without ice** (phrase)　去冰

14. **cocktail mixer** (n.)　調酒器

15. **drain** (vi.)　排掉水

C : Ok. So, that'll be two large, cold, but without ice, sugar-free, white Boba milk tea.

C : Ok. That'll be $140, please.

M : Here you are. (Michelle handed the cashier $140)

C : Your number is 123.

*A **tea barista**[26] started making their bubble tea. A few minutes later…*

C : Number 123! [i] Would you like a bag?

M : Yes, please.

C : [j] That'll be an extra two dollars, please.

M : [k] Can you place them together, please?

C : Sure. Here's your receipt. Enjoy!

Q & A

1. What were Ken and Michelle doing before they decided to stop by at the Boba Tea Café?

_____

2. What are some of Boba Tea Café's customer's favorites?

_____

3. What did Michelle order?

_____

4. Why did the cashier recommend a sugar-free drink to Michelle?

_____

5. How much did they pay for the bag?

_____

Important!
Speaking Practice Exercise

Practice saying the below short sentences.

a. Can you recommend some of your customer's favorites?
你能推薦一些客戶特別喜愛的嗎？

b. What size would you like?
大小呢？

c. Would you like it hot or cold?
請問你要冰的還是熱的？

d. How much ice would you like?
冰度呢？

e. What's cold, but without ice?
甚麼是去冰？

f. How much sugar would you like?
甜度呢？

g. What about sugar-free?
無糖 , 好嗎？

h. I'll have the same.
給我來一份一樣的。

i. Would you like a bag?
需要袋子嗎？

j. That'll be an extra two dollars, please.
再跟你多收兩元。

k. Can you place them together, please?
麻煩把它們裝在一起。

---

16. **icy-cold** (adj.) 極冷的 / 冰冷的
    同 frosty
    反 boiling hot

17. **particular** (adj.) 特別的 / 獨特的

18. **sugar level** (n.) 糖份水準
    同 glucose level

19. **intake** (n.) 引入口 / 納入（數）量
    同 input
    反 output

20. **regular sugar** (phrase) 正常糖
    反 sugar free / sugarless

21. **less sugar** (phrase) 七分 / 少糖

22. **half sugar** (phrase) 五分 / 半糖

23. **a little sugar** (phrase) 三分 / 微糖
    同 one-third sugar

24. **sugar-free** (adj.) 無糖
    同 no sugar
    反 regular sugar

25. **I'm on a diet** (phrase) 我在減肥
    同 I'm trying to lose weight
    反 I'm trying to gain weight

26. **tea barista** (n.) 茶調理師
    （比較 : coffee barista）

Listen and fill in the blanks Track 31

Listen to the conversation and fill in the blanks.

1. The customer would like a large, hot, _____ black Boba milk tea.
2. The customer would like a medium, cold, but _____ , half-sugar, bubble milk tea.
3. The customer ordered two Extra Large, _____ ice, _____ sugar, green tea.
4. The total price of the drinks is _____ .
5. The cost of the bag is an extra two _____ .

What kind of toppings would you like in your bubble tea?

Match the pictures to the answers given below:

a. Grass jelly	b. Green bean	c. Black Boba	d. Coconut jelly
e. Red bean	f. White Boba	g. Pudding	h. Sweet potato balls

(1)_____

(2)_____

(3)_____

(4)_____

(5)_____

(6)_____

(7)_____

(8)_____

Listen and Pronounce Track 32

Listen to the audio first. Then, try pronouncing each one of types of tea and toppings.

A. Types of Tea　茶種類

• Fruit Tea 果茶	• Ceylon Black Tea 錫蘭紅茶	• Passion Fruit Green Tea 百香綠茶
• Jasmine Tea 茉莉花茶	• Plum Green Tea 梅子綠茶	• Pu'er / Pu-erh Tea 普洱茶
• Pekoe 白毫茶	• Light Oolong Tea 青茶	• Dong Ding Oolong Tea 凍頂烏龍茶

• Tie-Guan-Yin Tea 鐵觀音茶	• Four Season Oolong Tea 四季春茶	• Oriental Beauty Oolong Tea 東方美人茶
• White-tipped Oolong Tea 白毫烏龍茶	• Earl Grey French Blue Tea 法式藍伯爵茶	

B. Types of Toppings　加料

• Aloe Vera 蘆薈	• Black Boba / black pearls 黑波霸 / 黑珍珠	• Coconut jelly 椰果
• Coffee jelly 咖啡凍	• Grass jelly 仙草	• Green bean / Mung bean 綠豆
• Konjac jelly 寒天 (蒟蒻)	• Longan 桂圓	• Plum 梅子
• Pudding 布丁	• Rat noodles 粉條	• Red bean 紅豆
• Sweet potato balls 地瓜圓	• Taro balls 芋圓	• Tea jelly 茶凍
• White Boba / white pearls 白波霸 / 白珍珠		

Photographs

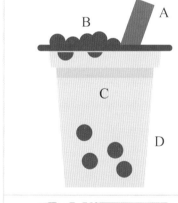

1. Name items A~D in the picture:

   A. _____

   B. _____

   C. _____

   D. _____

2. Which sentence best describes the picture?

   (A) A tea barista is making a cup of bubble tea.
   (B) A tea barista is calling out a customer's number.
   (C) A cashier is putting a customer's bubble tea into one bag.
   (D) A cashier is putting a customer's bubble tea into two separate bags.

   Your Answer: (　　)

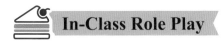

In-Class Role Play

Practice Role Play Exercise 1

- Using the below short conversation, ask each student to find a partner to practice with. One student plays the role of server (S), and the other, the customer (C).
- Then, change roles.

Practice Role Play Exercise 2

Now, practice again. This time, using the below menu, ask the students to replace the underlined words with items from the menu.

SHORT CONVERSATION PRACTICE

C : Customer　客戶
S : Server　服務生

S : How can I help you?
C : I'd like to a large green tea, please.
S : What kind of toppings would you like?
C : I'd to have big pearls, please.
S : Hot or cold?
C : Cold, please.
S : How much ice would you like? or How hot would you like your tea?
C : Cold, but without ice, please.
S : How much sugar would you like?
C : Half sugar, please.
S : That'll be $75.
C : Here you are.
　　{Ken handed the cashier $100}.
S : Here's your change. Your number is 123.

KOKO BUBBLE TEA ——— MENU ———

	M	L
Boba Milk Tea 波霸奶茶	70	80
Black Tea Macchiato 紅茶瑪奇朵	70	80
Bubble Green Milk Tea 珍珠奶綠	50	60
Bubble Milk Tea 珍珠奶茶	40	50
Coconut jelly bubble tea 椰果奶茶	50	60
Green Milk Tea 奶綠	50	60
Green Tea Latte 綠茶拿鐵	60	70
Hokkaido Milk Tea (Pudding & Pearl) 北海道布丁珍奶	90	100
Jasmine milk tea 茉莉奶茶	40	50
Lychee oolong tea 荔枝烏龍茶	60	70
Mango green tea 芒果綠茶	60	70
Matcha bubble milk tea 波霸抹茶拿鐵	70	80

	M	L
Matcha Latte 抹茶拿鐵	70	80
Milk tea 奶茶	50	60
Passion fruit green tea 百香綠茶	60	70
Peach black tea 水蜜桃紅茶	60	70
Pudding Milk Tea 布丁奶茶	60	70
Red Bean Milk Tea 紅豆奶茶	50	60
Roasted milk tea 烤奶茶	40	50
Taro bubble tea 芋頭珍珠奶茶	50	60
Taro milk tea 芋頭奶茶	60	70
Tea Latte 奶茶拿鐵	50	60
Winter melon mountain tea 冬瓜清茶	40	50

Regular ice 正常冰	Less ice 少冰	Half ice 半冰	A little ice 微冰	Cold, but without ice 去冰	Room temperature 常溫	Hot 熱的

100% Regular Sugar 正常糖	70% Less Sugar 七分 / 少糖	50% Half Sugar 五分 / 半糖	30% One-third sugar / A little sugar 三分 / 微糖	0% Sugar-free 無糖

Matcha bubble milk tea
波霸抹茶拿鐵

Coconut jelly bubble tea
椰果奶茶

Taro bubble tea
芋頭珍珠奶茶

Bubble milk tea
珍珠奶茶

Milk tea
奶茶

Winter melon mountain tea
冬瓜清茶

Unit 8

Wine
葡萄酒

Learning Objectives

What you will learn in this unit···
- Learn how to serve and order wine.
- Learn the different types of red wines and white wines.
- Learn about the major wine-producing countries in the world.
- Learn about the names of the major grapes used to produce wine.
- Learn what important verbs, phrases and vocabulary are used when serving wine.

Brainstorming

What does the type of wine you drink say about you?

☐ Red Wine - Pinot Noir
紅葡萄酒－黑比諾

☐ Red Wine - Cabernet Sauvignon
紅葡萄酒－卡本內蘇維翁

☐ Red Wine - Merlot
紅葡萄酒－梅洛

☐ White Wine - Chardonnay
白葡萄酒－霞多麗

☐ White Wine - Pinot Grigio
白葡萄酒－灰皮諾

☐ White Wine - Sauvignon
Blanc / 白葡萄酒－白蘇維翁

• •

1. What kinds of red wines do you know of, or drink?
2. What kinds of white wines do you know of, or drink?
3. Can you name some wine-producing countries?
   (Examples: France, Spain, Chile, etc.)
4. Ask your partner what is his/her favorite type of wine.

Wine Tasting Process　品酒過程

pour wine into a glass
倒酒到酒杯裡

open the wine with a wine opener
使用開瓶器開酒

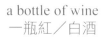

a bottle of wine
一瓶紅／白酒

vintage(2011)
葡萄收成年份

swirl the wine
搖酒(醒酒)

nod your head(means "yes")
點頭

a glass of wine
一杯紅／白酒

whiff
聞酒(將鼻子伸入杯中深呼吸)

shake your head(means "no")
搖頭

PRODUIT DE FRANCE

CHATEAV
◆ DE LA ◆
GALINIER
CÔTES DE PROVENCE
Appellation d'Origine contrôlée

2011
Vin de Provenc

Vincent Sauvestre, Propriétaire-Récoltant
hâteauneuf-le-Rouge, Bouches-du-Rhône, France

50 ML　　ALC. 11,5%

taste the wine / sip the wine
品酒／啜飲葡萄酒

stuck the cork back
把軟木塞塞進去

PREVIEW & IN CLASS PRACTICE

Practice Phrases

Work with a partner to practice saying the phrases below.

Making Requests – Customer	Making Offers – Server
We'd like to have some wine tonight. Can you give us the wine list? Can you give me the wine menu, please?	Sure. Here's our wine list. Here's the wine menu.
What red wine would you recommend?	Some of our favorite red wines are the Cabernet Sauvignon, Malbec, Merlot, Pinot Noir and Shiraz.
Can you recommend some white wines?	Some of our customers' favorites are the Chardonnay, Moscato, Pinot Grigio, Riesling and Sauvignon Blanc.
I'll have a glass of Chardonnay, please.	Sure.
I'll have a bottle of Merlot, please.	Great choice!

track 33

Listening Practice

Listen to the audio. Listen to the conversation between the server and customer, and then choose the correct answer.

1. ○ (A) The customer ordered a bottle of Malbec.
   ○ (B) The customer ordered a glass of Malbec.
2. ○ (A) The customer ordered a glass of Cabernet Sauvignon.
   ○ (B) The customer ordered a glass of Merlot.
3. ○ (A) The customer asked for red wine.
   ○ (B) The server recommended Chardonnay and Riesling.
4. ○ (A) The customer is American.
   ○ (B) The customer ordered a glass of Chardonnay.

*Steven and Penny decided to go for a **nightcap**[1] at a **wine bar**[2] after a long day at work.*

W：Waiter **S**：Steven **P**：Penny **Se**：Server

W：Good evening, ma'am. Good evening, sir. How are you doing tonight?

S ：Great! What about you?

P ：Wonderful! What about you?

W：How many people are there in your party tonight?

S ：Just two.

W：Ok. Please follow me.

The waiter brought Steven and Penny to their table.

Se：Good evening! I'm Betty, and I will be your server tonight.

S ：We'd like to have some wine tonight.

Se：Sure. ᵃ Here's our **wine list**[3].

S ：ᵇ What red wine would you recommend?

Se：ᶜ Some of our customers' favorites are the **Cabernet Sauvignon**[4], **Malbec**[5], **Merlot**[6], **Pinot Noir**[7] and **Shiraz**[8].

P ：I prefer white wine. Can you recommend some white wine?

Se：ᵈ Some of our customers' favorites are the **Chardonnay**[9], **Moscato**[10], **Pinot Grigio**[11], **Riesling**[12] and **Sauvignon Blanc**[13].

S ：Honey, what would you like? Red or white wine?

P ：ᵉ I'll have a glass of Chardonnay, please.

Se：What about for you, sir? What would you like?

S ：ᶠ I'll have a bottle of Merlot, please.

Se：Great choice!

The server returned with a bottle of French Merlot.

Se：Here you are, sir. This is a **French Merlot**[14] and the **vintage**[15] is 2015.

 New Words & Phrases   Track 35

1. **nightcap** (n.)　睡前酒
2. **wine bar** (n.)　葡萄酒酒吧
3. **wine list** (n.)　葡萄酒單
　　 wine menu
4. **Cabernet Sauvignon** (n.)　卡本內蘇維翁葡萄酒
5. **Malbec** (n.)　瑪律貝克葡萄酒
6. **Merlot** (n.)　梅洛葡萄酒
7. **Pinot Noir** (n.)　黑比諾葡萄酒
8. **Shiraz** (n.)　西拉葡萄酒
9. **Chardonnay** (n.)　霞多麗葡萄酒
10. **Moscato** (n.)　白莫斯卡托葡萄酒
11. **Pinot Grigio** (n.)　灰皮諾葡萄酒
12. **Riesling** (n.)　麗絲玲葡萄酒
13. **Sauvignon Blanc** (n.)　白蘇維翁葡萄酒
14. **French Merlot** (n.)　法國梅洛
15. **vintage** (adj.)　葡萄收成年分

*Then the server opened the bottle with a **wine opener**[16], and placed the **cork**[17] on the table. She **poured**[18] some red wine into Steven's wine glass and took a step back from him. Steven then picked up his wine glass, **swirled**[19] it a few times, then **stuck**[20] his nose all the way into it and took a big **whiff**[21]. Steven **nodded**[22] to the server. The server then poured another glass of wine for Penny.*

Se : Everything alright, sir? Ma'am?

S : Yes, it's perfect!

P : Yes, it's great! Thank you!

The server then poured Steven and Penny each glass of wine.

Q & A

1. What red wines did the server recommend?

   _____

2. What white wines did the server recommend?

   _____

3. What did Steven order?

   _____

4. Describe the bottle of wine that the server brought to Steven.

   _____

5. Describe the process of which the bottle of wine was served.

   _____

Important!
Speaking Practice Exercise

a. Here's our wine list.
   這是我們酒單。

b. What red wine would you recommend?
   你可以建議些紅酒嗎？

c. Some of our customers' favorites are the Cabernet Sauvignon, Malbec, Merlot, Pinot Noir and Shiraz.
   我們最受客戶歡迎有卡本內蘇維翁、瑪律貝克、梅洛、黑比諾及西拉。

d. Some of our customers' favorites are the Chardonnay, Moscato, Pinot Grigio, Riesling and Sauvignon Blanc.
   我們最受客戶歡迎的有霞多麗、白莫斯卡托、灰皮諾、麗絲玲、白蘇維翁。

e. I'll have a glass of Chardonnay, please.
   請給我一杯霞多麗葡萄酒。

f. I'll have a bottle of Merlot, please.
   請給我一瓶梅洛葡萄酒。

---

16. **wine opener** (n.)　開瓶器
    同 **bottle opener/corkscrew**
17. **cork** (n.)　軟木塞
18. **pour** (v.)　倒
19. **swirl** (v.)　輕搖酒杯
    同 **swoosh; spin around**
20. **stuck** (v.)　塞進去
    反 **unstuck**
    同 **cemented**

21. **whiff** (tr.v.)　輕輕的聞
    同 **inhale**
22. **nod your head** (phrasal verb)　點頭
    反 **shake your head**

Vocabulary Review

Antonym

1. white wine:_____
2. nod your head: _____
3. bottle: _____
4. stuck: _____

Synonym

1. wine list: _____
2. swirl the wine: _____
3. wine opener: _____
4. whiff: _____

Place the below wine tasting process in the correct order (1~6)

a. (   ) Taste the wine

b. (   ) Stuck the cork back into wine bottle

c. (   ) Whiff the wine

d. (   ) Pour wine into a glass

e. (   ) Swirl the wine

f. (   ) Open a bottle of wine with a wine opener/corkscrew

 Track 36

Listen and Pronounce

Listen to the audio first. Then, try pronouncing each one of the wines below.

• Cabernet Sauvignon 卡本內蘇維翁葡萄酒	• Malbec 瑪律貝克葡萄酒	• Merlot 梅洛葡萄酒	• Pinot Noir 黑比諾葡萄酒
• Shiraz 西拉葡萄酒	• Chardonnay 霞多麗葡萄酒	• Moscato 白莫斯卡托葡萄酒	• Pinot Grigio 灰皮諾葡萄酒
• Riesling 麗絲玲葡萄酒	• Sauvignon Blanc 白蘇維翁葡萄酒		

 Track 37

Listening Practice

Listen to the conversation and choose the correct answer.

1. (   ) a. The customer would like some red wine.

   (   ) b. The waiter recommended the Reisling and Moscato.

2. (   ) a. The customer ordered the Reisling and Moscato.

   (   ) b. The waiter recommended the Cabernet Sauvignon and Shiraz.

3. (   ) a. The lady ordered Chardonnay.

   (   ) b. The man ordered Chardonnay.

4. (   ) a. The customer prefers white wine.

   (   ) b. The server recommended French Merlot.

Photographs

Choose the answer that best describes the pictures.

1. (A) A woman is whiffing her wine.
   (B) A woman is tasting her wine.
   (C) A woman is swirling her wine.
   (D) A woman is pouring wine.

   Your answer: (   )

2. (A) It looks like a person is whiffing his/her wine.
   (B) It looks like a person is tasting his/her wine.
   (C) It looks like a person is swirling his/her wine.
   (D) It looks like a person is ordering a glass of wine.

   Your answer: (   )

3. Name the items (a) ~ (d) in the pictures below.

   (A) _____
   (B) _____
   (C) _____
   (D) _____

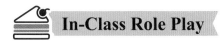

In-Class Role Play

Firstly, place the below sentences in the correct order. Then, using your answers, practice the conversation. One student plays the role of server, and the other, the customer. Using the below menu, try to order different types of wine. Replace the underlined words with different items on the menu. Practice as many times as possible, ordering different items from each menu above, and changing roles.

(   ) a.   I'll have a glass of Shiraz, please.

(   ) b.   Great choice! I'll be right back with your order.

(   ) c.   Sure. Here's our wine list.

(   ) d.   What red wine would you recommend?

(   ) e.   Good evening! I'm James, and I will be your server tonight.

(   ) f.   I'd like to have some red wine.

(   ) g.   Two of our favorite red wines are the Pinot Noir and Shiraz.

Wine

SPARKLING WINES	Glass	Bottle
Henkell Trocken Piccolo 200ml	-	8.5
Jindalee Brut Cuvee	7	25
Goodwyn Sparkling	5	22
Henkell Trocken	-	32
WHITE VARIETY		
Rascals Prayrt Verdelho	6	25
Goodness Estate Classic Dry White	6	25
RIESLING		
Spy Valley	7	25
Wolf Blass Yellow Label Riesling	6	22
Cookoothama Riesling	6	22
SAUVIGNON BLANC		
Barwang Semillon Sauvignon Blanc	7	26
Spy Valley Marlborough Sauvignon Blanc	7	28
Cookoothama Semillon Sauvignon Blanc	6	22
Nugan Estate Sauvignon Blanc	7	28
Goodwyn Semillon Sauvignon Blanc	5.5	22
CHARDONNAY		
Goodwyn Chardonnay	5.5	22
The Vines Chardonnay Semillon	5	20
Mortimers of Orange Chardonnay	5.5	22
Barwang Crisp Chardonnay	7	26
2 thumbs Chardonnay	7	26
Cookoothama Chardonnay	6	22
Barwang Chardonnay	7	26
SHIRAZ		
Cookoothama Shiraz	6	24
Barwang Shiraz Viognier	6.5	25
Mortimers of Orange	6	22
2 thumbs Shiraz	7	27
MERLOT & BLENDS		
Two Thumbs Cabernet Merlot	6	24
Goodness Estate Cabernet Merlot	6	24
Talinga Park Merlot	5.5	20
Barwang	7	26
CABERNET SAUVIGNON		
1828 Cab Sauvignon	6	24
Jim Barry Cover Drive	7	27

Unit 9

Learning Objectives

What you will learn in this unit…
- What are the top 15 countries with the most number of Michelin restaurants in the world?
- How to order Taiwanese night market food?
- Names of different Taiwanese night market food.
- What are the list of night market foods that made it to the Bib Gourmand list?

Brainstorming

How are Michelin stars defined?

☐ The Michelin Plate

☐ Michelin Bib Gourmand

☐ One Star Michelin Restaurants

☐ Two Star Michelin Restaurants

☐ Three Star Michelin Restaurants

1. What are the top 15 countries with the most number of Michelin restaurants in the world?
   (Example: madrid in Spain and Rome in Italy.)
2. What are some Michelin starred restaurants in Taipei? (Example: a-cut.)
3. Name some examples of Taiwanese night market food. (Example: shanghai steamed dumplings 小籠湯包)
4. Which city's night market have you been to before?
   (Example: Taipei city – Gong Guan night market 臺北市公館夜市)

KEY WORDS

Night Markets in Taipei city 台北市夜市

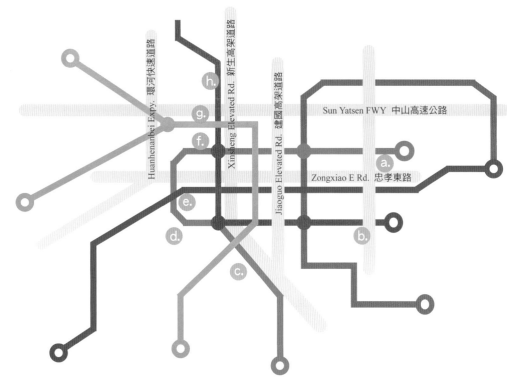

Huanhenanbei Expy. 環河快速道路
Xinsheng Elevated Rd. 新生高架道路
Jiaoguo Elevated Rd. 建國高架道路
Sun Yatsen FWY 中山高速公路
Zongxiao E Rd. 忠孝東路

a. Raohe night market 饒河夜市
b. Linjiang night market 臨江夜市
c. Gongguan night market 公館夜市
d. Nanjichang night market 南機場夜市
e. Huaxi night market 華西夜市
f. Ningxia night market 寧夏夜市
g. Yansan night market 延三夜市
h. Shilin night market 士林夜市

Steamed Pork Sandwich Ingredients 圖解割包

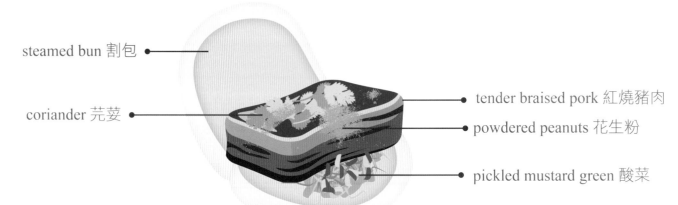

steamed bun 割包

coriander 芫荽

tender braised pork 紅燒豬肉

powdered peanuts 花生粉

pickled mustard green 酸菜

Street Foods on Bib Gourmand's List 台北米其林指南《必比登夜市小吃》

shredded chicken on rice
雞肉飯

sesame oil chicken
麻油雞

stinky tofu
臭豆腐

black pepper bun
胡椒餅

braised pork rice
滷肉飯

spareribs medicinal herbs stew
藥燉排骨

Shanghai-fried buns
上海生煎包

GUIDE MICHELIN

PREVIEW & IN CLASS PRACTICE

Practice Phrases

Work with a partner to practice saying the phrases below between a couple who are visiting a night market.

Michelle	Ken
• How many night markets are there in Taiwan?	• There are over 100 night markets in Taiwan.
• Wow! That's a lot! • How should we choose which one to go to?	• May I suggest that we try one that is listed in the Taipei Michelin Bib Gourmand?
• Great idea! Which night markets are on the Bib Gourmand list?	• Let me see… • (Ken started surfing the internet on his smartphone). • There's the Raohe night market, Tonghua night market, Ningxia night market, Shilin night market and Gongguan night market.
• Let's go to the nearest night market from here.	• Sounds good to me!
• Why don't we take a stroll through the street stalls first, and then see what we'd like to try out?	• Sounds like a great idea!
• There's braised pork rice, steamed pork sandwich, shredded chicken rice and stinky tofu.	• The steamed pork sandwich looks scrumptious. What is it?
• It's a fluffy, steamed white bun stuffed with tender braised pork, powdered peanuts, pickled mustard greens and coriander.	• Sounds delicious. • I'd like to try that.

Listening Practice   Track 38

Listen to the audio. Listen to the conversation between a couple who are visiting a night market.

1. ◯ (A) Ken and Michelle are planning to visit over 100 night markets in Taiwan that are on the Taipei Michelin Bib Gourmand list.

   ◯ (B) Ken and Michelle are planning to visit a night market in Taiwan that is listed in the Taipei Michelin Bib Gourmand.

2. ◯ (A) Ken and Michelle are planning to visit the Raohe night market which is the nearest night market from where they are.

   ◯ (B) Ken and Michelle are planning to visit a night market which is nearest to them.

3. ◯ (A) Ken said that the steamed pork sandwich looks scrumptious.

   ◯ (B) Ken said that the braised pork rice looks scrumptious.

4. ◯ (A) Ken and Michelle ordered two steamed pork sandwiches for $100.

   ◯ (B) Ken and Michelle ordered one steamed pork sandwiches for $100.

5. ◯ (A) The total price of the two bowls of sesame oil chicken is $380.

   ◯ (B) The total price of the two bowls of sesame oil chicken is $400.

Ken and Michelle are discussing which night market[1] to visit tonight.

M：Michelle　　K：Ken　　V1：Vendor1　　V2：Vendor2

M：^a<u>How many night markets are there in Taiwan?</u>

K：^b<u>There are over 100 night markets in Taiwan.</u>

M：Wow! That's a lot! How should we choose which one to go to?

K：May I suggest that we try one that is listed in the **Taipei Michelin Bib Gourmand**[2]?

M：Great idea! ^c<u>Which night markets are on the Bib Gourmand list?</u>

K：Let me see… (*Ken started surfing the internet on his smartphone*).
　　^d<u>There's the **Raohe night market**[3], **Tonghua night market**[4],
　　Ningxia night market[5], **Shilin night market**[6] and **Gongguan night market**[7].</u>

M：Let's go to the nearest night market from here.

K：Sounds good to me!

Ken and Michelle arrived at the Ningxia night market.

M：Why don't we **take a stroll**[8] through the **street stalls**[9] first, and then see what we'd like to try out?

K：^e<u>Sounds like a great idea!</u>

M：There's **braised pork rice**[10], **steamed pork sandwich**[11], **shredded chicken rice**[12] and **stinky tofu**[13].

K：^f<u>The steamed pork sandwich looks **scrumptious**[14]. What is it?</u>

M：It's a **fluffy,**[15] steamed white bun **stuffed**[16] **with tender braised pork**[17], **powdered peanuts**[18], **pickled**[19] **mustard greens**[20] and **coriander**[21].

K：^g<u>Sounds delicious. I'd like to try that.</u>

 New Words & Phrases Track 40

1. **night market** (n.)　夜市
   同 (open air market)

2. **Michelin Bib Gourmand** (n.)
   米其林指南《必比登夜市小吃》

3. **Raohe night market** (n.)　饒河街夜市

4. **Tonghua night market** (n.)　通化街夜市

5. **Ningxia night market** (n.)　寧夏夜市

6. **Shilin night market** (n.)　士林夜市

7. **Gongguan night market** (n.)　公館夜市

8. **take a stroll** (vi.)　閑逛 / 漫步 / 慢慢地走
   同 walk slowly / linger　反 scurry

9. **street stalls** (n.)　街頭小吃攤
   反 restaurant

10. **braised pork rice** (n.)　滷肉飯

11. **steamed pork sandwich** (n.)　割包
    同 Taiwanese hamburger

12. **shredded chicken rice** (n.)　雞肉飯

13. **stinky tofu** (n.)　臭豆腐

14. **scrumptious** (adj.)　美味的
    同 yummy / appetizing　反 yukky / distasteful

15. **fluffy** (adj.)　蓬鬆的
    同 soft　反 firm

16. **stuffed with** (phrasal verb)　塞滿…
    把佐料（紅燒豬肉、花生粉、醃的芥末菜、新鮮香菜）塞進（蒸包）里。
    同 filled with something, especially of poultry and other food

17. **tender braised pork** (n.)　紅燒豬肉

18. **powdered peanuts** (n.)　花生粉

19. **pickled** (n.)　醃的

20. **pickled mustard green** (n.)　酸菜

21. **coriander** (n.)
    芫荽（香菜英文是 parsley，另一種香菜英文是 coriander，這兩種香菜是不同的植物）
    同 parsley

Ken and Michelle joined the queue. It was finally their turn.

M : [h] Can I have two steamed pork sandwiches, please?

V1[22]: $140, please.

M : Here you are.

  {*Michelle handed $200 to the vendor*}.

V1: $60 is your change.

  {*The vendor then handed them* two steamed pork sandwiches}.

M : Here you are.

  (*The vendor* **handed**[23] *them two steamed pork sandwiches*).

Ken and Michelle started strolling through the street stalls again.

K : There's the **Shanghai pan-fried buns**[24], **spareribs**[25] **medicinal herbs**[26] **stew**[27,28,] **black pepper bun,**[29] **sesame oil chicken**[30] and **beef noodle soup**[31].

M : The sesame oil chicken smells delicious. What's in it?

K : It's chicken cooked in sesame oil and ginger **broth**[32]. It's usually eaten during the winter to keep your body warm. Would you like to try it?

M : Sure. [i] My mouth is watering already!

K : [j] Can I have two **bowls**[33] of sesame oil chicken, please?

V2: That'll be $380.

K : Here's $400.

V2: $20 is your **change**[34]. [k] Please find a table and we'll send your food over.

22. **vendor** (n.) 小販
    同 hawker 反 customer

23. **handed** (adj.) 遞…/用 ... 手的

24. **Shanghai pan-fried buns** (n.) 上海生煎包

25. **spareribs** (n.) 排骨

26. **medicinal herbs** (n.) 藥草 / 藥材 / 卓藥

27. **stew** (v.) 燉
    同 simmer, braise, stew slowly

28. **spareribs medicinal herbs stew** (n.) 藥燉排骨

29. **black pepper bun** (n.) 胡椒餅

30. **sesame oil chicken** (n.) 麻油雞

31. **beef noodle soup** (n.) 牛肉麵

32. **broth** (n.) 清湯 / 湯
    同 puree / light soup

33. **bowl** (n.) 碗
    同 dish

34. **change** (n.) 找零頭 / 零錢
    反 bill / dollar

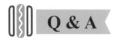

Q & A

1. Which type of night market did Ken and Michelle decide to go to?

   _____

   _____

2. Name four street foods that Ken and Michelle first came across.

   _____

   _____

3. What street food did Ken and Michelle decide to try first?

   _____

   _____

4. Name some other street foods Ken and Michelle came across after trying the steamed pork sandwich.

   _____

   _____

5. How much is one bowl of sesame oil chicken?

   _____

   _____

Important!
Speaking Practice Exercise

Practice saying the below short sentences.

a. How many night markets are there in Taiwan?
   台灣有多少個夜市？

b. There are over 100 night markets in Taiwan.
   台灣有超過 100 個夜市。

c. Which night markets are on the Bib Gourmand list?
   米其林必比登（Bib Gourmand）推薦的夜市有哪些？

d. There's the Raohe night market, Tonghua night market, Ningxia night market, Shilin night market and Gongguan night market.
   有饒河夜市、通化夜市、寧夏夜市、士林夜市和公館夜市。

e. Sounds like a great idea!
   這主意聽起來很不錯！

f. The steamed pork sandwich looks scrumptious.
   割包看起來很美味。

g. Sounds delicious. I'd like to try that.
   聽起來很好吃，我想嘗試一下。

h. Can I have two steamed pork sandwiches, please?
   請給我兩個割包。

i. My mouth is watering already!
   我已經在流口水了！

j. Can I have two bowls of sesame oil chicken, please?
   請給我兩碗麻油雞。

k. Please find a table and we'll send your food over.
   請先找位子坐，我會把菜送過去。

Surf the Internet Exercise

Check online as to which night market food, and the name of the night market that made it to the Bib Gourmand list lately? You may surf the Internet to find your answers.

List of Bib Gourmand foods in Taipei 台北米其林指南《必比登夜市小吃》

Name of night market food	Name of night market
Example: Lan Chia steamed pork sandwich 藍家割包	Example: Gongguan night market 公館夜市
1.	
2.	
3.	
4.	
5.	

Listen and fill in the blanks

 Track 41

Listen to the conversation and fill in the blanks.

1. Ken suggested to Michelle that they try a night market that is listed on the Taipei _____ _____ Gourmand.

2. Ken and Michelle decided to take a _____ through the street stalls at the Ningxia night market first and see what they'd like to try out.

3. The steamed pork sandwich is a fluffy, steamed white bun stuffed with tender _____ _____, powdered peanuts, pickled mustard greens and coriander.

4. When Ken and Michelle strolled through the street stalls, they saw Shanghai _____-_____ buns, spareribs medicinal herbs stew, black pepper bun, sesame oil chicken and _____ _____ soup.

5. The sesame oil chicken is cooked in sesame oil and ginger _____. It's usually eaten during the winter to keep your body warm.

Track 42

Listen and Pronounce

Listen to the audio first. Then, try practicing how to pronounce each of night market foods.

• beef noodles 牛肉麵	• black pepper bun 胡椒餅	• braised dishes 滷味
• braised pork rice 滷肉飯	• coffin bread / deep-fried coffin-shaped sandwich 棺材板	• Danzai noodles (Ta-a noodles) 擔仔麵
• goose meat 鵝肉	• grilled squid 烤魷魚	• Oden 關東煮

• oyster omelet 蚵仔煎	• oyster vermicelli 蚵仔麵線	• pan-fried buns 生煎包
• rice pudding 碗粿	• squid thick soup/squid potage 魷魚羹	• sticky rice sausage 大腸包小腸
• stinky tofu 臭豆腐	• Taiwanese-style fried chicken 鹹酥雞	• tempura 甜不辣
• tube rice pudding 筒仔米糕		

Picture-Vocabulary Review

Match the pictures to the answers given below:

a. One Star Michelin Restaurant	b. Michelin Bib Gourmand	c. Two Star Michelin Restaurant
d. Three Star Michelin Restaurant	e. The Michelin Plate	

(1)_____ (2)_____ (3)_____ (4)_____ (5)_____

Photographs

1. Which one of the following best describes the picture?

   (A) Some people are strolling at a night market.
   (B) Some vendors are strolling at a night market.
   (C) Some people are looking for a table at a night market.
   (D) Some people are ordering food from a vendor at a night market.

   Your answer: (   )

2. Which one of the following best describes the picture?

   (A) A vendor is handing food to a person at a night market.
   (B) A person is handing money to a vendor at a night market.
   (C) A vendor is ordering food at a night market.
   (D) A person is ordering food at a night market.

   Your answer: (   )

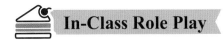 **In-Class Role Play**

Practice Role Play Exercise 1

• Using the below short conversation, ask each student to find a partner to practice with. One student plays the role of server (S), and the other, the customer (C).

• Then, change roles.

Practice Role Play Exercise 2

• Now, practice again. This time, using the below menu, ask the students to replace the underlined words with items from the menu.

SHORT CONVERSATION PRACTICE

C1, C2 : **Customer 1, Customer 2** （客戶 1, 客戶 2）
V1, V2 : **Vendor 1, Vendor 2** （小販 1, 小販 2）

Michelle (C1) and Ken (C2) are visiting a night market. Below is a conversation between two customers (C1, C2) and two night market vendors (V1, V2).

1. C1 : Can I have <u>two</u> <u>steamed pork sandwiches</u>, please?
2. V1 : <u>$140</u>, please.
3. C1 : Here you are.
   {Ken handed $200 to the vendor}.
4. V1 : $60 is your change.
   {*The vendor then handed them <u>two</u> <u>steamed pork sandwiches</u>*}.

   {*Ken and Michelle started strolling through the street stalls again*}.

4. C2 : Can I have <u>two bowls</u> of <u>sesame oil chicken</u>, please?
5. V2 : That'll be <u>$380</u>.
6. C2 : Here's <u>$400</u>.
7. V2 : <u>$20</u> is your change. Please find a table, and we'll send it over.

   {*Ken and Michelle found a table and sat down to wait for their food*}.

NIGHT MARKET MENU

Steamed pork sandwich
割包　$80

Stinky tofu
臭豆腐　$70

Braised dishes
滷味　$30 each

Braised pork rice
滷肉飯　$40

Taiwanese mega-dumpling (Ba Wan)
肉圓　$50

Fish ball soup
魚丸湯　$75

Oyster vermicelli
蚵仔麵線　$70

Goose meat
鵝肉　$150

Sausage
香腸　$30 each

Tube rice pudding
筒仔米糕　$60

Pig's blood rice pudding
豬血糕　$35 / Stick

Tamsui deep fried tofu pockets
淡水阿給　$50

Slack season Danzai noodles
擔仔麵　$70

Tempura
甜不辣　$20 each

Unit 10

Ice-cream
冰淇淋

Learning Objectives

What you will learn in this unit···
- How to serve ice-cream.
- How to order ice-cream.
- Popular ice-cream flavors.
- Popular ice-cream toppings.
- Ice-cream-related keyword verbs, phrases and idioms.

Brainstorming

What does your favorite ice-cream flavor say about you?

☐ Vanilla
香草口味

☐ Cotton candy
棉花糖冰淇淋

☐ Strawberry sorbet
草莓雪酪

☐ Chocolate chip
巧克力脆片冰淇淋

☐ Almond ice-cream
杏仁冰淇淋

1. What is your favorite ice-cream flavor?(Examples: vanilla, chocolate, etc.)
2. Which is your favorite ice-cream parlor?(Example: Häagen-Dazs.)
3. What is your favorite ice-cream brand? (Example: Meiji.)
4. What is your favorite ice-cream topping?(Examples: M&M's, chocolate chips, etc.)
5. Ask your partner what ice-cream flavor and topping he/she likes.

KEY WORDS

Toppings 加在冰淇淋上面的配料

caramel syrup
焦糖糖漿

oreo
奧利奧

TOPPINGS

bubble gum
泡泡糖

marshmallow
棉花糖

whpped cream
鮮奶油

bananas
香蕉

gummy bears
小熊軟糖

chocolate chips
巧克力碎片

chocolate sauce /
syrup
巧克力糖漿

peanut butter cup
花生杯

coconut
椰子

Butter finger
巧克力糖

three scoops / triple scoop
三球冰淇淋

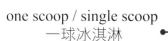
one scoop / single scoop
一球冰淇淋

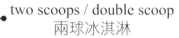
two scoops / double scoop
兩球冰淇淋

sample ice-cream
冰淇淋樣品

ice-cream parlor
冰淇淋商店

vanilla ice-cream
香草冰淇淋

chocolate chip
ice-cream
巧克力脆片冰淇淋

86
in a cone
裝在甜筒裡

in a cup
裝在杯子裡

sorbet / sherbet
雪酪

mango sorbet
芒果雪酪

PREVIEW & IN CLASS PRACTICE

Practice Phrases

Work with a partner to practice saying the phrases below.

Making Offers – Server	Making Requests – Customer
Would you like to try a sample?	Can I try the cotton candy, please? Can I try the mango sorbet, please? Can I try the almond, please?
Would you like to try another sample?	Can I try the coffee, please? Can I try the vanilla, please? Can I try the blueberry, please?
How many scoops would you like?	One scoop, or single scoop, please. Two scoops, or double scoop, please. Three scoops, or triple scoop, please.
Would you like it in a cup or cone? In a cup or cone?	In a cone/cup, please. Cone/cup, please. I'd like it in a cup/cone, please.
Would you like any toppings on your ice-cream?	Chocolate chips, please. M&M's, please. Gummy bears, please.

 track 43

Listening Practice

Listen to the audio. Listen to the conversation between the server and customer, and then choose the correct answer.

1. ○ (A) The server offered a sample ice-cream to the customer.
   ○ (B) The customer requested a sample of ice-cream from the server.
2. ○ (A) The customer wants to try the chocolate flavor.
   ○ (B) The customer wants to try the chocolate chip flavor.
3. ○ (A) The server asked if the customer would like to pay now.
   ○ (B) The server asked if the customer would like to try another sample.
4. ○ (A) The customer wants to try the strawberry ice-cream.
   ○ (B) The customer wants to buy the strawberry ice-cream.

*Penny and Michelle are waiting in line at the H-D **ice-cream parlor**[1].*

S：Server   P：Penny   M：Michelle

S : How can I help you?

P : (to Michelle) Wow! There are so many different **flavors**[2]!

M : I know. I don't know what to choose!

S : [a] <u>Would you like to try a **sample**[3]?</u>

P : Can I have a sample of the **cotton candy**[4]?

S : Sure, here you are.

*The server **scooped**[5] some cotton candy ice-cream using a **tiny**[6] **plastic spoon**[7] and handed it to Penny.*

S : Here you are.

P : (to Michelle) [b] <u>This is not really my taste.</u>

S : [c] <u>Would you like to try another sample?</u>

P : Can I try the **mango sorbet**[8, 9], please?

The server scooped some mango sorbet using a tiny plastic spoon.

S : Here you are.

P : (to Michelle) Hmmm… This is delicious!

Penny liked the mango sorbet that she tried.

P : [d] <u>Can I have two scoops, please?</u>

S : [e] <u>Would you like it in a cup or **cone**[10]?</u>

P : In a cone, please.

S : [f] <u>Would you like any **toppings**[11] on your ice-cream?</u>

P : Yes. Can I have the **chocolate chip**[12] and **M&M's**[13], please?

S : Sure. Here you are.

 New Words & Phrases Track 45

1. **ice-cream parlor** (n.)　冰淇淋商店

2. **flavors** (n.)　口味
    同 tastes

3. **sample** (n.)　樣品
    同 try/test

4. **cotton candy** (n.)　棉花糖冰淇淋

5. **scoop** (vt.)　用勺舀（或指舀一勺）

6. **tiny** (adj.)　極小的、微小的
    反 huge/giant

7. **plastic spoon** (n.)　塑膠湯匙

8. **mango sorbet** (n.)　芒果雪酪

9. **sorbet** (n.)　雪酪
    同 sherbet

10. **cone** (n.)　甜筒
    反 cup

11. **toppings** (n.)　加在冰淇淋上面的配料

12. **chocolate chip** (n.)
    巧克力脆片冰淇淋（加在冰淇淋上面的配料）

13. **M&M's** (n.)
    美國的牛奶巧克力品牌，M&M 巧克力（加在冰淇淋上面的配料）

It was now Michelle's turn to order.

S : Would you like to try a sample?

M : Can I try the coffee, please?

S : Sure. Here you are.

Michelle didn't look very satisfied, so the server asked again.

S : Would you like to try another sample?

M : Can I try the **vanilla**[14], please?

S : Sure, here you are.

The server scooped some vanilla ice-cream using a tiny plastic spoon and handed it to Michelle.

S : Here you are.

M : (to Penny) Hmmm... I love it!

M : Can I have two **scoops**[15] of vanilla ice-cream, please?

S : Would you like it in a cup or cone?

M : In a cup, please.

S : Would you like any toppings?

M : **Gummy bears**[16], please.

S : Great choice! Are you paying together?

P : Yes, we are.

S : $10.50, please.

P : Here's the **exact change**[17].

Important!
Speaking Practice Exercise

a. Would you like to try a sample?
你想試吃嗎？

b. This is not really my taste.
這不太合我口味。

c. Would you like to try another sample?
請問你想再試吃其他口味嗎？

d. Can I have two scoops, please?
請給我兩球冰淇淋。

e. Would you like it in a cup or cone?
請問你要裝在杯子還是甜筒裡呢？

f. Would you like any toppings on your ice-cream?
請問你想加點配料嗎？

 Q & A

1. What sample did Penny first try?
_____

2. What was the second sample that Penny tried?
_____

3. How did Penny want her ice-cream served?
_____

4. What samples did Michelle try?
_____

5. How many scoops of ice-cream did Michelle want, and how did she want it?
_____

14. **vanilla** (n.) 香草冰淇淋

15. **scoop** (n.) 一 / 兩 / 三球冰淇淋
- one scoop = single scoop 一球冰淇淋
- two scoops = double scoop 兩球冰淇淋
- three scoops = triple scoop 三球冰淇淋

16. **gummy bears** (n.)
小熊軟糖（加在冰淇淋上面的配料）

17. **exact change** (n.) 正確的數目 / 恕不找零

Listen and fill in the blanks

Listen to the conversation and fill in the blanks.

1. The server offered the customer to try a _____.

2. The customer ordered two scoops of _____-flavored ice-cream in a _____.

3. The customer wants two _____ of strawberry ice-cream.

4. The customer wants her ice-cream in a _____.

5. The customer would like _____ topping on her ice-cream.

Listening Practice

 Track 47

Listen to the audio. Listen to what the server and customer want, and then choose the correct answer.

1. (   ) (A) The customer tried the strawberry flavor ice-cream.

   (   ) (B) The customer tried the strawberry sorbet ice-cream.

2. (   ) (A) The customer tried another free sample of vanilla ice-cream.

   (   ) (B) The customer decided to buy two scoops of vanilla ice-cream.

3. (   ) (A) The customer wanted her ice-cream in a cone.

   (   ) (B) The customer wanted her ice-cream in a cup.

4. (   ) (A) The customer ordered chocolate chips ice-cream.

   (   ) (B) The customer ordered chocolate chips toppings
   for her ice-cream.

Listen and Pronounce

Track 48

Listen to the audio first. Then, try pronouncing each one of the ice-cream flavors below.

• Cappuccino ice-cream 卡布奇諾冰淇淋	• Caramel ice-cream 焦糖冰淇淋	• Cheesecake ice-cream 起司蛋糕冰淇淋
• Melon ice-cream 哈密瓜冰淇淋	• Peach ice-cream 水蜜桃冰淇淋	• Blueberry ice-cream 藍莓冰淇淋
• Chocolate chip ice-cream 巧克力脆片冰淇淋	• Cotton candy ice-cream 棉花糖冰淇淋	• Cream soda ice-cream 蘇打冰淇淋
• Hazelnut chocolate ice-cream 榛果巧克力冰淇淋	• Mango sorbet 芒果雪酪冰淇淋	• Matcha ice-cream 抹茶冰淇淋
• Mint chocolate ice-cream 薄荷巧克力冰淇淋	• Tiramisu ice-cream 提拉米蘇冰淇淋	• Vanilla ice-cream 香草冰淇淋

Photographs

Choose the answers that best describes the pictures.

1. (A) There are two scoops of ice-cream in a cup.
   (B) This is a triple scoop ice-cream in a cup.
   (C) This is a double scoop ice-cream in a cone.
   (D) There are three scoops of ice-cream in a cone.

   Your answer: (   )

2. (A) It looks like someone is scooping ice-cream into a cup.
   (B) It looks like someone is scooping ice-cream into a cone.
   (C) It looks like someone is putting a topping onto an ice-cream.
   (D) It looks like someone is trying a sample of ice-cream.

   Your answer: (   )

 In-Class Role Play

Firstly, place the below sentences in the correct order. Then, using your answers, practice the conversation. One student plays the role of server, and the other, the customer. Using the below menu, try to order different types of ice-cream flavors and toppings. Replace the underlined words with different words. Practice as many times as possible, ordering different items from each menu above, and changing roles.

(   ) a. I'd like one scoop of cotton candy, please.

(   ) b. Would you like it in a cup or cone?

(   ) c. Sure. Here you are!

(   ) d. Your total will be $3.00, please.

(   ) e. I'd like it in a cone, please.

(   ) f. Can I help you? Would you like to try a sample?

(   ) g. Can I have a try the cotton candy, please?

(   ) h. Hmm··· This is delicious!

(   ) i. Here you are.
           Keep the change!

(   ) j. Would you like
           any toppings?

(   ) k. Can I have M&M's, please?

(   ) l. Thank you. Have a great day!

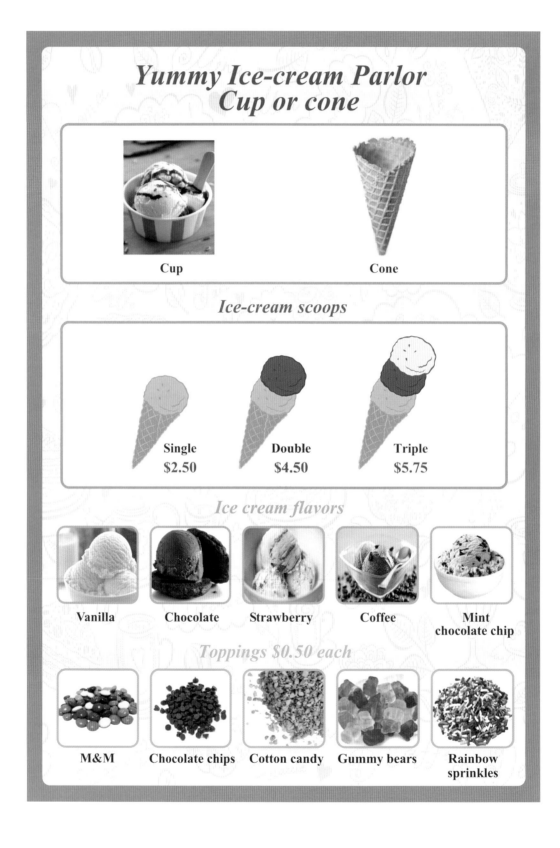

Yummy Ice-cream Parlor
Cup or cone

Cup

Cone

Ice-cream scoops

Single
$2.50

Double
$4.50

Triple
$5.75

Ice cream flavors

Vanilla

Chocolate

Strawberry

Coffee

Mint
chocolate chip

Toppings $0.50 each

M&M

Chocolate chips

Cotton candy

Gummy bears

Rainbow
sprinkles

Unit 11

At a Steakhouse
在牛排館

Learning Objectives

What you will learn in this unit…
- How to serve steak at a steakhouse.
- How to order steak at a steakhouse.
- Names of different types of steaks such as Filet Mignon and Ribeye steak.
- What is means by "how would you like your steak done?"
- Keyword verbs, phrases and idioms used at a steakhouse.

Brainstorming

What does your steak choice say about you?

☐ Filet Mignon /
菲力牛排

☐ Ribeye steak /
肋眼牛排

☐ New York Strip /
紐約客牛排

☐ T-Bone steak /
丁骨牛排

☐ Sirloin steak /
沙朗牛排

1. What is your favorite type of steak?
   (Examples: Filet Mignon, Ribeye, etc.)
2. How do you like your steak?
   (Examples: medium-rare, medium, etc.)
3. What is your favorite steakhouse?
4. Ask your partner what his/her favorite type of steak is, and how he/she likes his/her steak.

Types of Steak 牛排名稱與部位

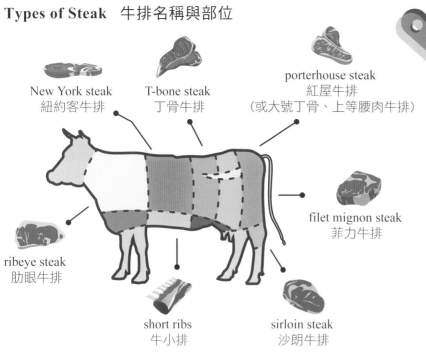

New York steak
紐約客牛排

T-bone steak
丁骨牛排

porterhouse steak
紅屋牛排
（或大號丁骨、上等腰肉牛排）

filet mignon steak
菲力牛排

ribeye steak
肋眼牛排

short ribs
牛小排

sirloin steak
沙朗牛排

How would you like your steak? 你的牛排要幾分熟？

rare 一分熟 · Cool and soft with red center.

medium-rare 三分熟 · Warm and slightly firm with red center.

medium 五分熟 · Warm and firm with pink center.

medium-well 七分熟 · Very warm and firm with a slight pink center.

well-done 全熟 · Very warm and quite firm with a brown center.

Sides 配菜

clam chowder
蛤蜊巧達濃湯

vegetable soup
蔬菜湯

onion soup
洋蔥湯

french fries
薯條

baked potato(with sour cream)
烤馬鈴薯（含酸奶）

mashed potatoes
馬鈴薯泥

PREVIEW & IN CLASS PRACTICE

Practice Phrases

Work with a partner to practice saying the phrases below.

Making Requests – Customer	Making Offers – Server
What would you like for your entrée?	I'd like a Ribeye steak, please. I'd like a T-bone steak, please. I'd like a New York Strip, please. I'd like a Sirloin steak, please.
How would you like your steak?	Rare, please.（一分熟） Medium-rare, please.（三分熟） Medium, please.（五分熟） Medium-well, please.（七分熟） Well-done, please.（全熟）
Would you like fries, baked potatoes or mashed potatoes with your entrée?	Fries, please. Baked potato, please. Mashed potatoes, please.
Would you like sour cream on your baked potato?	"Yes, please", or "No, thanks"
Would you like some soup or salad?	Soup, please. Salad, please.
What kind of soup would you like?	Onion soup, please. Clam chowder, please. Vegetable soup, please.
What kind of salad would you like?	Caesar salad, please. Chicken salad, please. Grilled chicken salad, please.

Track 49

Listening Practice

Listen to the audio. Listen to the conversation between the hostess and customer, and then choose the correct answer.

1. ○ (A) The customer would like to go to New York.
   ○ (B) The customer would like to order a New York Strip.
2. ○ (A) The customer wants his steak medium-rare.
   ○ (B) The customer wants his steak rare.
3. ○ (A) The customer wants mashed potatoes.
   ○ (B) The customer wants a baked potato.
4. ○ (A) The customer ordered a clam chowder.
   ○ (B) The customer ordered an onion soup.

Unit 11　At a Steakhouse 在牛排館

CONEVRSATION

*Steven and Penny are going on a date at the **Oak**[1] **Steakhouse**[2].*

S：Steven　　Se：Server　　P：Penny

Se：Good evening! I'm Jane, and I'll be your server for tonight. Just want to let you know that we have a special for tonight. You can choose the **Filet Mignon**[3], **Ribeye**[4] or **T-bone**[5] steak. The special also comes with a soup or salad. Take your time on the menu, and I'll be back to take your orders.

Steven and Penny started looking at the menu…

P：The special sounds really good, but it doesn't have my favorites --- the **New York Strip**[6] or **Sirloin steak**[7].

S：Well, you don't have to order the specials.

P：Anyway, the specials sound too much for me. I think I'll just have a New York strip and a **clam chowder**[8].

S：I'll have the special. It has the Filet Mignon which is my favorite.

Steven signaled to the server.

Se：Are you ready to order now?

S：Yes, we are.

Se：What would you like for your **entrée**[9], ma'am?

P：I'd like a New York steak, please.

Se：Ok. How would you like your steak?

P：**Medium-rare**[10], please.

Se：Very good choice. Would you like some soup or salad with that?

P：I'll just have a clam chowder, please.

Se：Would you like a **baked potato**[11] or **mashed potatoes**[12]?

P：No, thanks. No, thanks. I'll just have the steak and clam chowder, please.

Se：And, for you, sir?

S：I'd like to have the special, please.

Se：[a] <u>What would you like for your entrée?</u>

 New Words & Phrases Track 51

1. **oak** (n.)　橡樹
2. **steakhouse** (n.)　牛排館
3. **Filet Mignon** (n.)　菲力牛排
4. **Ribeye steak** (n.)　肋眼牛排
5. **T-bone steak** (n.)　丁骨牛排
6. **New York Strip** (n.)　紐約客牛排
7. **Sirloin steak** (n.)　沙朗牛排

8. **clam chowder** (n.)　蛤蜊巧達濃湯
9. **entrée** (n.)　主菜
   同 main dish
10. **medium-rare** (as in steak) (v.)　三分熟
11. **baked potato** (n.)　烤馬鈴薯
12. **mashed potatoes** (n.)　馬鈴薯泥

S : I'd like the Filet Mignon, please.

Se : [b] How would you like your steak?

S : I'd like it **medium**[13], please.

Se : [c] Would you like a baked potato or mashed potatoes?

S : I'll have the baked potato, please.

Se : [d] Would you like **sour cream**[14] on that?

S : Yes, that'll be wonderful.

Se : Your special comes with a soup or salad. [e] Would you like soup or salad?

S : I'll have an **onion soup**[15], please.

Se : Very well. I'll be back with your orders!

Q & A

1. Give a reason why Penny did not order the special.

   _____

2. What did Penny order?

   _____

3. How did Penny want her steak?

   _____

4. What did Steven order?

   _____

5. How did Steven want his steak?

   _____

Important!
Speaking Practice Exercise

a. What would you like for your entrée?
   請問你想點什麼主菜呢？

b. How would you like your steak?
   你的牛排要幾分熟？

c. Would you like a baked potato or mashed potatoes?
   您要烤馬鈴薯還是馬鈴薯泥呢？

d. Would you like sour cream on that (baked potato)?
   你要加點酸奶嗎？

e. Would you like soup or salad?
   您要沙拉或湯呢？

---

13. medium (as in steak) (v.)　五分熟

14. sour cream (n.)　酸奶

15. onion soup (n.)　洋蔥湯

Practice Writing and Saying

Answer the following questions "how you would like your steak," and then practice saying them with a partner.

Rare　一分熟　————————

Cool and soft with red center.

Medium-rare　三分熟　————————

Warm and slightly firm with red center.

Medium　五分熟　————————

Warm and firm with pink center

Medium-well　七分熟　————————

Very warm and firm with a slight pink center.

Well-done　全熟　————————

Very warm and quite firm with a brown center.

Example

Server: How would you like your steak?

Customer: <u>Rare, please</u>. （一分熟）

Exercise

1. Server: How would you like your steak?
   Customer: _____, _____. （三分熟）

2. Server: How would you like your steak?
   Customer: _____, _____. （五分熟）

3. Server: How would you like your steak?
   Customer: _____, _____. （七分熟）

4. Server: How would you like your steak?
   Customer: _____, _____. （全熟）

Listen and fill in the blanks　Track 52

Listen to the conversation and fill in the blanks.

1. The customer ordered a _____ steak.
2. The customer ordered a _____ steak
3. The customer wants his steak _____.
4. The customer wants his steak _____.
5. The customer ordered an _____ soup.

Photographs

Look at the pictures at match it with the answers given below.

a. filet mignon	b. baked potato with sour cream	c. grilled chicken
d. T-bone steak	e. vegetable soup	f. clam chowder

1. _____

2. _____

3. _____

4. _____

5. _____

6. _____

 In-Class Role Play

Firstly, place the below sentences in the correct order. Then, using your answers, practice the conversation. One student plays the role of server, and the other, the customer. Using the below menu, try to order different types of steaks and soups. Replace the underlined words with different words. Practice as many times as possible, ordering different items from each menu above, and changing roles.

(   ) a.   <u>Onion soup</u>, please.

(   ) b.   Very well. I'll be back with your orders!

(   ) c.   Are you ready to order?

(   ) d.   <u>Medium-rare</u>, please.

(   ) e.   Would you like a baked potato or mashed potatoes?

(   ) f.   Would you like sour cream on that?

(   ) g.   <u>Yes</u>, please.

(   ) h.   Would you like soup or salad?

(   ) i.   I'd like a <u>Ribeye steak</u>, please.

(   ) j.   How would you like your steak?

(   ) k.   I'll have the <u>baked potato</u>, please.

(   ) l.   Yes, I am.

(   ) m.   What would you like for your entrée?

Jim's Steakhouse

★ How would you like your steak? ★

RARE Cool and soft with red center.

MEDIUM-RARE Warm and slightly firm with red center.

MEDIUM Warm and firm with pink center.

MEDIUM-WELL Very warm and firm with a slight pink center.

WELL-DONE Very warm and quite firm with a brown center.

★ Steaks ★

Filet Mignon

Ribeye Steak

New York Strip

T-Bone Steak

Sirloin Steak

★ Sides ★

Mashed potatoes

Baked potato with sour cream

Fries

★ Salads ★

Caesar salad

Chicken salad

★ Soups ★

Clam chowder

Onion soup

Chicken soup

Tomato soup

Vegetable soup

Unit 12

Donuts
甜甜圈

Learning Objectives

What you will learn in this unit⋯
- Did you know that some countries have their own special donut?
- Learn about the names of some notable donut shops and their countries of origin.
- How to take an order for donuts?
- Learn about the different types, flavors and fillings for donuts.

Brainstorming

Did you know that some countries have their own special type of donut?

☐ Cruller / 可麗露 (France)

☐ BeaverTails / 海狸尾 (Canada)

☐ Churros / 吉拿棒 (Spain, Mexico)

☐ Beignets / 麵包圈 (France)

☐ Youtiao / 油條 (China, Asia)

1. Can you name some other different types of donuts around the world? (Example: An-donut (Japan).)
2. Guess which country eats the most donuts? Then, surf the internet to find out the correct answer! Google Keywords: Which country eats the most donuts?
3. Ask your partner what is his/her favorite type of donut?

KEY WORDS

Donuts 甜甜圈

original glazed donuts
經典糖霜甜甜圈

assorted variety donuts
綜合口味甜甜圈

Festive Donuts 節慶甜甜圈

tree of hope donut
希望之樹甜甜圈

rubies and pearls donut
紅寶石和珍珠甜甜圈

Tiramisu cake donut
提拉米蘇蛋糕甜甜圈

Santa belly donut
聖誕老人肚皮甜甜圈

Rudolph donut
魯道夫甜甜圈

Number of donuts 甜甜圈數量

one / single
一個

half dozen donuts (6 donuts)
半打甜甜圈（6入）

one dozen donuts (12 donuts)
一打甜甜圈（12入）

debit card 簽帳金融卡 /
credit card 信用卡

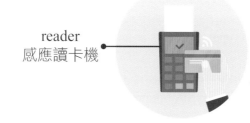

reader
感應讀卡機

tap-to pay
(tap-and go / contactless payment)
零接觸支付服務

PREVIEW & IN CLASS PRACTICE

Popular Donuts From Around the World

 甜甜圈介紹

Look at the pictures, and then write down the name of the donut and its country of origin. Scan the below QRCODE to find your answers for the below exercise.

1. Name of donut: B_____
   Origin: G_____

2. Name of donut: B_____
   Origin: C_____

3. Name of donut: C_____
   Origin: S_____

4. Name of donut: F_____
   Origin: C _____

5. Name of donut: F_____
   Origin: A_____

6. Name of donut: Z_____
   Origin: I_____

Practice Phrases

Work with a partner to practice saying the phrases below between a server and a customer at a donut shop.

Server	Customer
• Next! Merry Christmas, folks! • Can I help you?	• Merry Christmas to you too! • We'd like to have half a dozen original glazed donuts, one dozen assorted variety donuts and one dozen festive donuts, please.
• Okay. What kinds of assorted varieties would you like? • Do you want to pick the same varieties or different varieties for each box?	• The same varieties would be fine.
• Okay. What would you like? • The server then passed the donuts to the cashier…	• Can I have … • two glazed vanilla cake donuts, • two matcha stripes donuts, • two strawberry iced with sprinkles, • two original glazed donuts, • two peanut butter iced glazed donuts and • two salted caramel donuts, please?

Listening Practice

 Track 53

Listen to the audio. Listen to the conversation between the order-taker/server and the customer, and then choose the correct answer.

1. ◯ (A) Ken and Michelle are picking up donuts at Donut Hole for their Christmas party tomorrow.
   ◯ (B) Ken and Michelle are picking up donut holes for their Christmas party tomorrow.
2. ◯ (A) Ken and Michelle are going to get a dozen original glazed donuts.
   ◯ (B) Ken and Michelle are going to get half a dozen original glazed donuts.
3. ◯ (A) The customer ordered four glazed vanilla cake pronuts.
   ◯ (B) The customer ordered two glazed vanilla cake donuts and two matcha stripes donuts.
4. ◯ (A) The customer ordered two strawberries and two peanut butter iced glazed donuts.
   ◯ (B) The customer ordered two strawberry iced with sprinkles and two peanut butter iced glazed donuts.
5. ◯ (A) The customer paid using his debit card.
   ◯ (B) The customer paid using his credit card.

Track 54

*It's Christmas Eve. Michelle and Ken are planning to have some friends over for a Christmas party the next day. They are **lining up**[1] at the Donut Hole to **pick up**[2] some **donuts**[3] for their Christmas party tomorrow.*

K：Ken　M：Michelle　S：Server　C：Cashier

K：Honey, how many donuts do you think we should get for our party tomorrow?

M：Let's see… [a] How many guests are we **having over**[4]?

K：There's Christina, Justin, Janet, Sam, Britney… **Hmmm**[5]… About 20 people.

M：What about two to three dozen donuts?

K：[b] Sounds good to me!

Ken started looking at the menu on the wall.

K：Honey, they have **original**[6] **glazed**[7] donuts and **assorted**[8] **variety**[9] **donuts**[10].

M：I'd like to get **at least**[11] a box of **festive**[12] donuts.

K：I agree!

M：Honey, look at how cute the **Santa's Belly**[13] and **Rudolph**[14] donuts are!

K：I **bet**[15] that will definitely **pump up the Christmas spirit**[16]!

M：And, get everyone into a **festive mood**[17] too!

K：So, honey, what do you think we should get?

M：What about **half a dozen**[18] original glazed donuts, **one dozen**[19] assorted variety donuts and one dozen festive variety donuts?

K：Sounds great to me!

 New Words & Phrases Track 55

1. **lining up** (n.)　排隊
   同 queuing up　反 splitting up

2. **pick up** (phrasal verb)　買東西 / 撿起、拾起（某物）/ 得病
   同 buy　反 sell

3. **donuts** (n.)　甜甜圈
   同 doughnuts)
   Doughnut 或 donuts? 後者更常用。甜甜圈在英文裡為 doughnut，來自 dough 加上 nut。Dough 指的是「麵團」，而 nut 描述過去甜甜圈的形狀。以前的甜甜圈並不是「圈」，而是現在所説的甜甜圈球，大小和一個 nut 差不多，而 nut 即指「堅果、果仁」，doughnut 經演變，已非小球狀，而是現在所見的圈狀食物。

4. **having over / have over** (vt.)
   邀請…來家裡作客

5. **Hmmm…** (exclamation)
   嗯【説話時停頓或表示不確定】

6. **original** (adj.)　經典 / 原味
   同 classic

7. **glazed donut** (n.)　糖霜甜甜圈。
   同 coated
   圈外面會裹上一層薄薄的糖霜，糖霜乾掉後會呈現閃亮、光滑的樣子，因糖霜遇冷會形成脆硬的口感，加上內層柔軟的甜甜圈，整體吃起來外酥內軟。

8. **assorted** (adj.)　什錦的 / 各種各樣（混在一起）
   同 mixed　反 same

9. **variety** (n.)　各種各樣
   同 assortment　反 homogeneous / sameness

10. **assorted variety donuts** (n.)　綜合口味甜甜圈

11. **at least** (phrase)　至少
    同 more than / no less than

12. **festive** (adj.)　節慶
    同 jovial / Christmassy　反 gloomy / joyless

It was Ken and Michelle's turn.

S : Next! Merry Christmas, **folks**[20]! [c] <u>Can I help you?</u>

K : Merry Christmas to you too! [d] <u>We'd like to have half a dozen original glazed donuts, one dozen assorted variety donuts and one dozen festive donuts, please.</u>

S : Okay. [e] <u>What kinds of assorted varieties would you like?</u>
  [f] <u>Do you want to pick the same varieties or different varieties for each box?</u>

M : [g] <u>The same varieties would be fine.</u>

S : Okay. What would you like?

M : Can I have two **glazed vanilla cake donuts**[21], two **matcha stripes donuts**[22], two **strawberry iced with sprinkles**[23], two **original glazed donuts**[24], two **peanut butter iced glazed donuts**[25] and two **salted caramel donuts**[26], please?

The server then passed the donuts to the cashier…

C : That'll be $5.99 (five, ninety-nine) for half a dozen glazed donuts, $9.99 (nine, ninety-nine) for a dozen assorted variety donuts and $10.99 (ten, ninety-nine) for a dozen festive donuts.
  [h] <u>Your total comes up to $26.97 (twenty-six, ninety-seven).</u>
  [i] <u>Will that be **debit**[27] or **credit**[28]?</u>

K : Debit, please.

C : Just place your card on the **reader**[29] and **tap-to-pay**[30].

[*Beep!*]

C : Okay. [j] <u>You may remove your card now.</u>

{*Ken removed his card from the reader.*}

C : [k] <u>Would you like a paper bag?</u>

K : [l] <u>No thanks. I brought my own bag.</u>

C : Here you go! Merry Christmas!

Ken and Michelle (together): Merry Christmas to you too!

---

13. **Santa's Belly** (n.) 聖誕老人肚皮
14. **Rudolph** (n.) 魯道夫。
   紅鼻子馴鹿魯道夫（Rudolph the red-nosed reindeer）是一隻虛構的馴鹿。 牠有一個發光的紅鼻子，常被稱為「聖誕老人的第九隻馴鹿」，是在平安夜為聖誕老人拉雪橇的帶頭馴鹿。 牠鼻子發出的亮光能夠在風雪中照亮全隊所走的路。
15. **I bet** (phrase) 我打賭 / 我敢斷定 / 我確信
16. **Pump up the Christmas spirit** (phrase) 提升耶誕氣氛
   同 Light up the Christmas spirit
   反 Dampen the Christmas spirit
17. **festive mood** (phrase) 節日氣氛
   同 joyful spirit
18. **half a dozen** (n./ adj.) 半打（6 入）
   同 six / 6 / half-dozen
19. **one dozen** (n./ adj.) 一打（12 入）
   同 twelve / 12
20. **folks** (n.) 人們〔古、方〕
   同 people(口語) 家屬 / 親戚 (古語) 民族 / 種族

21. **glazed vanilla cake donuts** (n.) 香草糖霜蛋糕甜甜圈
22. **matcha stripes donuts** (n.) 抹茶甜甜圈
23. **strawberry iced with sprinkles** (n.) 繽紛草莓甜甜圈
24. **original glazed donuts** (n.) 經典糖霜甜甜圈
   反 assorted variety donuts
25. **peanut butter iced glazed donuts** (n.) 花生糖霜甜甜圈
26. **salted caramel donuts** (n.) 海鹽焦糖甜甜圈
27. **debit** (card) (n.) 簽帳金融卡
   反 credit card
28. **credit** (card) (n.) 信用卡
   反 debit card
29. **reader** (n.) 感應讀卡機
30. **tap-to-pay** (phrase) 零接觸支付也被稱為『一拍即付』
   同 contactless payment / tap-and-go

Q & A

1. Why did Michelle and Ken want to buy donuts?

   _____

   _____

2. Can you name five guests who were coming to Ken and Michelle's Christmas party?

   _____

   _____

3. What types of donuts did Donut Hole offer?

   _____

   _____

4. How many donuts is half a dozen?

   _____

   _____

5. How many and what types of donuts did Ken and Michelle decide to get?

   _____

   _____

6. What was the total price of the donuts?

   _____

   _____

Important!
Speaking Practice Exercise

Practice saying the below short sentences.

a. How many guests are we having over?
   我們要邀請多少客人來家裡？

b. Sounds good to me!
   聽起來很不錯！

c. Can I help you?
   你需要什麼服務嗎？

d. We'd like to have half a dozen original glazed donuts, one dozen assorted variety donuts and one dozen festive donuts, please.
   我們想要半打經典糖霜甜甜圈，一打綜合口味甜甜圈，還有一打節慶甜甜圈。

e. What kinds of assorted varieties would you like?
   你想要什麼綜合口味甜甜圈呢？

f. Do you want to select the same varieties or different varieties for each box?
   你想要挑選每盒相同或不相同口味的甜甜圈呢？

g. The same varieties would be fine.
   每一盒都一樣的口味就可以了。

h. Your total comes up to $26.97 (twenty-six, ninety-seven).
   總共是 26.97 美元。

i. Will that be debit or credit?
   你要使用簽帳金融卡或信用卡呢？

j. You may remove your card now.
   你可以把卡片拿起來了。

k. Would you like a paper bag?
   你需要個紙袋嗎？

l. No thanks. I brought my own bag.
   不，謝了。我有自備袋子。

Listen and fill in the blanks

Track 56

Listen to the conversation and fill in the blanks.

1. Michelle and Ken are l_____ u_____ at the Donut Hole to _____ _____ p_____
   u_____ some donuts for about 20 people for their Christmas party tomorrow.

2. Donut Hole offers o_____ glazed donuts and a_____ variety donuts.

3. The customer would like to order two g_____ vanilla cake donuts and two m_____ stripes donuts.

4. The customer would like to order two strawberry iced with s_____ and p_____ b_____ iced glazed donuts

5. The customer paid using his _____ card by placing his card on the _____.

Mix & Match the pictures with the words given below:

a. 繽紛巧克力甜甜圈 Chocolate Iced With Sprinkles Donut
b. 經典糖霜甜甜圈 Original Glazed Donut
c. 草莓夾心貝 Strawberry Filled Donut
d. 繽紛草莓甜甜圈 Strawberry Iced With Sprinkles Donut
e. 杏仁白巧克力甜甜圈 Almond White Chocolate Donut
f. 抹茶甜甜圈 Matcha Stripes Donut
g. 海鹽焦糖甜甜圈 Salted Caramel Donut

(1)_____ (2)_____ (3)_____

(4)_____ (5)_____ (6)_____

Listen and Pronounce

Track 57

Listen to the audio, and then try to pronounce each one of the following types of donut.

• Almond White Chocolate Donuts 杏仁白巧克力甜甜圈	• Chocolate Iced Glazed Donuts 巧克力糖霜甜甜圈	• Chocolate Iced With Sprinkles Donuts 繽紛巧克力甜甜圈
• Chocolate Walnuts Cake Donuts 核桃巧克力蛋糕	• Cinnamon Sugar Donuts 肉桂糖甜甜圈	• Glazed Chocolate Cake Donuts 巧克力糖霜蛋糕
• Glazed Vanilla Cake Donuts 香草糖霜蛋糕	• Matcha Stripes Donuts 抹茶甜甜圈	• Nutty Cocoa Ring Donuts 榛果脆脆甜甜圈
• Original Glazed Donuts 經典糖霜甜甜圈	• Peanut Butter Iced Glazed Donuts 花生糖霜甜甜圈	• Salted Caramel Donuts 海鹽焦糖甜甜圈
• Strawberry Filled Donuts 草莓夾心貝	• Strawberry Iced Glazed Donuts 草莓糖霜甜甜圈	• Strawberry Iced With Sprinkles Donuts 繽紛草莓甜甜圈

Number, Prices & Calculations

Based on the below menu, count the total number of donuts and total price of the donuts based on the following #Customer Orders 1,2 and 3, and then write down your answers in the given boxes.

TYPE OF DONUT	HALF DOZEN	DOZEN	ONE / SINGLE
ORIGINAL GLAZED DONUTS	$5.99	$8.99	$0.99
ASSORTED VARIETY DONUTS	$6.99	$9.99	$1.09
FESTIVE VARIETY DONUTS	$7.99	$10.99	$1.29

Example:

I'd like to have half a dozen original glazed donuts, one dozen assorted variety donuts and half a dozen festive donuts, please.

Type of donut	Number of donuts	Price for each type of donut
Original glazed donuts	6	$5.99
Assorted variety donuts	12	$9.99
Festive donuts	6	$7.99
Total number of donuts	**24 donuts**	
Total price of donuts		**$23.97**

1. # Customer Order 1

I'd like to have a dozen original glazed donuts, two dozen assorted variety donuts and half a dozen festive donuts, please.

Type of donut	Number of donuts	Price for each type of donut
Original glazed donuts		$
Assorted variety donuts		$
Festive donuts		$
Total number of donuts	**donuts**	-
Total price of donuts		$

2. # Customer Order 2

I'd like to have three original glazed donuts, half a dozen assorted variety donuts and one dozen festive donuts, please.

Type of donut	Number of donuts	Price for each type of donut
Original glazed donuts		$
Assorted variety donuts		$
Festive donuts		$
Total number of donuts	**donuts**	-
Total price of donuts		$

3. # Customer Order 3

I'd like to have three dozen original glazed donuts and one dozen festive donuts, please.

Type of donut	Number of donuts	Price for each type of donut
Original glazed donuts		$
Assorted variety donuts		$
Festive donuts		$
Total number of donuts	**donuts**	-
Total price of donuts		$

Photographs

1. Write down the names of the festive donuts shown in the picture:

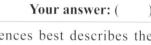

(A) R_____ donut
(B) T_____ donut
(C) R_____ donut
(D) T_____ donut
(E) S_____ donut

Your answer: (   )

2. Which of the following sentences best describes the picture?

(A) A person is entering a 4-digit pin number on a reader.
(B) A person is signing his/her name on a reader.
(C) A person is tapping to pay on a reader.
(D) A person is swiping his/her credit card on a reader.

Your answer: (   )

In-Class Role Play

Practice Role Play Exercise 1

- Using the below short conversation, ask each student to find a partner to practice with. One student plays the role of server (S), and the other, the customer (C).
- Then, change roles.

Practice Role Play Exercise 2

- Now, practice again. This time, using the below menu, ask the students to replace the underlined words with items from the menu.

SHORT CONVERSATION PRACTICE

G：**Guest**　客戶
S：**Server**　服務生
C：**Cashier**　收銀員

S : Next! Can I help you?

G : Hi! We'd like to have <u>half a dozen</u> <u>original glazed donuts</u>, please.

S : Anything else?

G : No, that'll be all.

S : Okay. [*The server then passed the donuts to the cashier*].

C : Your total comes up to <u>$5.99 (five, ninety-nine)</u>.
　　Will that be debit or credit?

G : <u>Debit</u>, please.

C : Just place your card on the reader and tap-to-pay.
　　[Beep!]

C : Okay. You may remove your card now.
　　[*Ken removed his card from the reader*].

C : Do you need a bag?

G : <u>No, thanks</u>.

C : Here you go.
　　[*The cashier handed the donuts to the customer*].

G : Thank you.

C : Have a nice day!

DONUT MENU

TYPE OF DONUT	HALF DOZEN	DOZEN	ONE / SINGLE
ORIGINAL GLAZED DONUTS	$5.99	$8.99	$0.99
ASSORTED VARIETY DONUTS	$6.99	$9.99	$1.09
FESTIVE DONUTS	$7.99	$10.99	$1.29

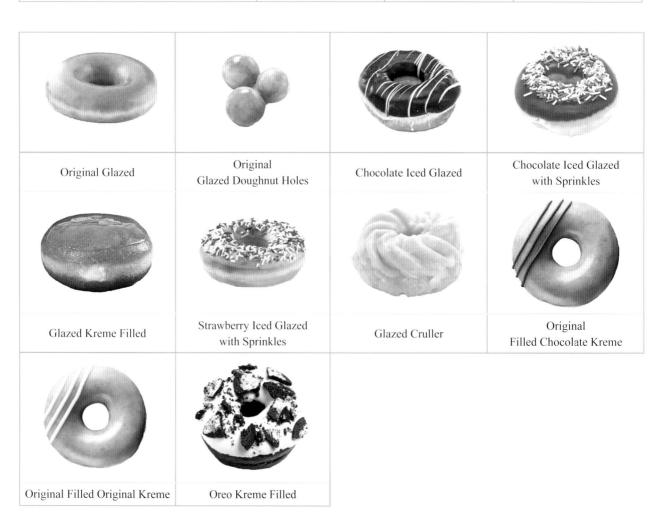

Original Glazed

Original Glazed Doughnut Holes

Chocolate Iced Glazed

Chocolate Iced Glazed with Sprinkles

Glazed Kreme Filled

Strawberry Iced Glazed with Sprinkles

Glazed Cruller

Original Filled Chocolate Kreme

Original Filled Original Kreme

Oreo Kreme Filled

FESTIVE DONUTS

國家圖書館出版品預行編目 (CIP) 資料

餐飲英文 / 鄭寶菁編著 . -- 五版 . -- 新北市：
　全華圖書 , 2024.02
　　　面；　公分
　　ISBN 978-626-328-767-9（平裝）

1. 英語 2. 會話 3. 餐飲業

805.188　　　　　　　　　　112017972

餐飲英文

作　　者 / 鄭寶菁

發 行 人 / 陳本源

執行編輯 / 黃艾家

封面設計 / 盧怡瑄

出 版 者 / 全華圖書股份有限公司

郵政帳號 / 0100836-1號

印 刷 者 / 宏懋打字印刷股份有限公司

圖書編號 / 0821504

五版一刷 / 2024年2月

定　　價 / 450元

Ｉ Ｓ Ｂ Ｎ / 978-626-328-767-9（平裝）

全華圖書 / www.chwa.com.tw

全華科技網 Open Tech / www.opentech.com.tw

若您對書籍內容、排版印刷有任何問題，歡迎來信指導book@chwa.com.tw

臺北總公司（北區營業處）

地址：23671新北市土城區忠義路21號

電話：(02) 2262-5666

傳眞：(02) 6637-3695、6637-3696

南區營業處

地址：80769高雄市三民區應安街12號

電話：(07) 381-1377

傳眞：(07) 862-5562

中區營業處

地址：40256臺中市南區樹義一巷26號

電話：(04) 2261-8485

傳眞：(04) 3600-9806

REVIEW & IN CLASS PRACTICE

Unit 1   Restaurant Reservations & Corkage Fees

Test Yourself

Fill in the blanks with the correct answers:

| a. hold your reservation | b. corkage | c. make a reservation |
| d. private room | e. hold the line | f. cellphone |

1. A : Good afternoon, Bubba Gum restaurant. This is Samantha.
      How may I help you?
    B : Yes, I'd like to make a_____.
    A : Sure. When would you like to make reservation for?
    B : July 2nd for ten people, please.

2. A : Alright. So, that'll be a party of ten. What time will that be?
    B : Seven-thirty in the evening (7:30 p.m.).
    A : Ok. Is there anything else I can help you with?
    B : Can I have a _____ , please?
    A : Just give me a moment, please. Let me check.
      Please_____.
    B : Sure.
    A : Yes, we have a private room available for July 2nd at 7:30 p.m.
    B : That sounds great!

3. A : Can I have your name and _____ number, please?
    B : Sure. My name is Ken Jordan, and my cellphone number is 0983-112-310.
    A : Okay, Mr. Jordan. We have a private room for ten at 7:30 p.m. on July 2nd.
      Is that correct?
    B : Yes, that's right.

4. A : We will _____for fifteen minutes.
      Please arrive before 7:15 p.m.
    B : Sure. I'll be there before 7:15.

5. A : Anything else I can help you with?
    B : Yes. We will be celebrating one of our friend's birthday on that day. So, I was wondering if we could bring our own wine?
    A : We charge a _____ fee of $10 per bottle of wine.
    B : Ok, got it!

Q & A

Go to the conversation part of this unit. After listening and reading the conversation, answer the following questions:

1. Which restaurant did Ken want to make a reservation for?

_____

2. What date and time did Ken want to make a reservation?

_____

3. What does "how many in your party" mean?

_____

4. What is Ken's full name and cellphone number?

_____

5. How long will Bubba Gum restaurant hold Ken's reservation?

_____

Match the Chinese-English Translations

a. 坐在吸煙區
b. 外帶
c. 食物外送
d. 得來速
e. 坐在噴泉旁或靠近噴泉
f. 坐在庭院
g. 坐吧台
h. 坐在非吸煙區
i. 休閑餐廳
j. 靠窗
k. 戶外用餐
l. 餐車
m. 精緻餐飲
n. 速食店
o. 坐在包廂內

1. (　　) Takeout / Takeaway
2. (　　) Food delivery
3. (　　) Drive-thru'
4. (　　) Outdoor dining
5. (　　) Food truck
6. (　　) Fine dining restaurants
7. (　　) Fast food restaurants
8. (　　) Casual dining restaurants
9. (　　) By the window
10. (　　) By the fountain area or near the fountain area
11. (　　) By the patio
12. (　　) At the bar
13. (　　) In the non-smoking section
14. (　　) In the smoking section
15. (　　) private room / VIP room / booth / private area / private section

Where would you like to be seated?

Fill in the blanks using the choices given below:

Types of seating available in a restaurant:

(a) by the window
(b) by the fountain area
(c) near the fountain area
(d) by the patio
(e) at the bar
(f) in a quiet area
(g) in the non-smoking section
(h) in the smoking section
(i) in a private room / private area / private section / booth / VIP room
(j) outdoors

Example 1 – Server asks 服務生詢問顧客

Server: Where would you like to sit?
Customer: I'd like to sit by the window, please.

Example 2 – Customer requests 顧客要求座位

Customer: Can I sit by the window, please?
Server: Sure. Just give me a moment.

1. Server: Where would you like to sit?
    Customer: I'd like to sit _____, please.
2. Customer: Can I sit _____, please?
    Server: Sure. Just give me a moment.
3. Server: Where would you like to sit?
    Customer: I'd like to sit _____ , please.
4. Customer: Can I sit _____, please?
    Server: Sure. Just give me a moment.
5. Server: Where would you like to sit?
    Customer: I'd like to sit _____ , please.
6. Customer: Can I sit _____, please?
    Server: Sure. Just give me a moment

Choose the incorrect answer:

1. (　　) Where would you like to be seated?

   (A) By the ratio　(B) By the bar area　(C) In a VIP room　(D) Near the fountain area.

2. (　　) Ways to buy food:

   (A) takeaway　(B) drive out　(C) food truck　(D) food delivery.

3. (　　) People who work at a restaurant:

   (A) waitress　(B) host　(C) server　(D) VIP.

4. (　　) Types of restaurants/eateries:

   (A) fine dining restaurant　(B) casual dining restaurant　(C) hot restaurant　(D) sandwich bar.

5. (　　) Types of restaurants/eateries:

   (A) bakery café　(B) drive-thru'　(C) food truck　(D) steak.

REVIEW & IN CLASS PRACTICE

Unit 2

Test Yourself

a. refillable	b. fountain	c. coleslaw	d. medium
e. wedges	f. pieces	g. recipe	h. family

1. A: Next! Can I take your order?
   B: I'd like to have ten _____ of chicken and two large Cokes, please.
2. A: What _____ would you like?
   B: I'd like the original flavor, please.
3. C: Next! Can I take your order?
   D: I'd like to have the ten-piece _____ meal, please.
4. C: You can choose two sides. What would you like?
   D: I'd like a _____ and _____, please.
5. D: What would you like to drink?
   C: I'd like a _____ Pepsi, please.
   D: Sure.
6. C: Are the drinks _____?
   D: Yes. You may refill by the soda _____ right by the corner.
   C: That sounds great!

Match the questions with the answers given below

a. popcorn nuggets	b. original	c. mashed potatoes
d. chicken wings	e. chicken drumsticks	f. wedges
g. corn	h. grilled	i. chicken drummettes
j. biscuits	k. coleslaw	l. spicy
m. chicken thigh		

1. Chicken recipes / flavors
   (1) _____
   (2) _____
   (3) _____
2. Parts of chicken
   (1) _____
   (2) _____
   (3) _____
   (4) _____

3. Sides

    (1) _____

    (2) _____

    (3) _____

    (4) _____

    (5) _____

    (6) _____

Sentence Practice

Rewrite the below sentences in the correct orders.

1. meal / like / try / family/ you / would / to / our / ?

    _____?

2. value / way/ get / you / more / this

    _____.

3. original / spicy / like / our / would / recipe / you / try / to / or / ?

    _____?

4. sides / like / you / would / of / kind / what / ?

    _____?

5. refillable / drinks / the / are / ?

    _____?

Choose the right answer

Which of the following is the incorrect answer?

1. (   ) Parts of a chicken:

    (A) sticks   (B) chicken wings   (C) chicken thigh   (D) chicken drumlets.

2. (   ) Parts of a chicken:

    (A) chicken drumsticks   (B) chicken breast   (C) chicken drummettes   (D) chicken nuggets.

3. (   ) Sides:

    (A) fries   (B) wedges   (C) spicy   (D) mashed potatoes.

4. (   ) Chicken recipes:

    (A)original   (B) Mexico   (C) spicy   (D)crispy.

5. (   ) Items in a family meal:

    (A) chicken   (B) fries   (C) coleslaw   (D) original.

REVIEW & IN CLASS PRACTICE

Unit 3 Traditional Taiwanese Breakfast

Test Yourself

Fill in the blanks with the correct answers:

a. cutlery	b. turnip cake	c. pair of chopsticks
d. fifty-five	e. soybean milk	

1. On Saturday morning, Ken, Michelle and Penny decided to have a local breakfast together. They visited a local Taiwanese breakfast shop, called Soy Milk Shop.
    Server   : Good morning. Are you ready to order?
    Customer : Yes, I am. I'll have a _____ with thick soy sauce and chili sauce, please.
    Server   : Would you like to add an egg?
    Customer : Yes, please.
2. Server   : Would you like anything to drink?
    Customer : I'll have a hot _____, please.
    Server   : Is that all?
    Customer : Yes, that'd be all.
3. Cashier   : Your total will be _____, please.
    Customer : Here you go.
4. Cashier   : Would you like any _____?
    Customer : A _____and a straw, please.
    Cashier   : Sure. Here's your change.

Q & A

Go to the conversation part of this unit. After listening and reading the conversation, answer the following questions:

1. How much did Ken pay for his breakfast?

    _____

2. What kind of cutlery did Ken ask for?

    _____

3. What did Michelle order?

    _____

4. How much did Michelle give the cashier?

    _____

5. How much is Michelle's change?

    _____

6. How much is Penny's breakfast?

    _____

Mix and Match the Chinese-English Translations

a. 紫米飯糰

b. 米漿

c. 蛋餅

d. 找零錢

e. 醬油膏

f. 辣椒醬

g. 醬油

h. 蘿蔔糕

i. 熱豆漿

j. 餐具 / 餐飲用具

k. 糯米

l. 一龍小籠湯包

1. (   ) turnip cake

2. (   ) hot soybean milk

3. (   ) cutlery

4. (   ) change

5. (   ) glutinous rice

6. (   ) Taiwanese sweet glutinous rice roll

7. (   ) rice & peanut milk

8. (   ) Taiwanese omelet

9. (   ) chili sauce

10. (   ) soy sauce

11. (   ) thick soy sauce

12. (   ) steamed pork buns in a bamboo steamer

Ordering Traditional Taiwanese Breakfast

Example:

I'd like to have a <u>clay oven roll with an egg</u>, and a <u>hot soybean milk</u>, please.

(A1/A2/A3)   (B)   (B)

1. I'd like to have a _____ and _____ _____ ,please.

(A1/A2/A3)   (B)   (B)

2. I'd like to have a _____ and _____ _____ ,please.

(A1/A2/A3)   (B)   (B)

3. I'd like to have a _____ and _____ _____ ,please.

(A1/A2/A3)   (B)   (B)

4. I'd like to have a _____ and _____ _____ ,please.

(A1/A2/A3)   (B)   (B)

5. I'd like to have a _____ and _____ _____ ,please.

(A1/A2/A3)   (B)   (B)

(A) Taiwanese Breakfast Food

- Clay oven roll (with or without egg) 燒餅 (夾蛋 / 不要夾蛋)
- Flaky scallion pancake 蔥抓餅
- Pork bun 肉包
- Vegetable bun 菜包
- Turnip cake / Radish cake (with chili sauce / with thick soy sauce) 蘿蔔糕 （ 加辣椒 / 加醬油膏 ）
- Steamed pork buns in a bamboo steamer (10 pieces) 一龍小籠湯包 （ 10 粒 ）
- Scallion pancake 蔥油餅
- Steamed bun (with or without egg) 饅頭 (夾蛋 / 不要夾蛋)
- Taiwanese sweet glutinous rice roll 紫米飯糰
- Taiwanese glutinous rice roll 飯糰
- Sweet potato congee 地瓜稀飯
- Taiwanese omelet 蛋餅
- Thin green onion cake with twisted cruller 煎餅油條
- Twisted cruller / fried bread stick 油條
- Salted soymilk 鹹豆漿

(B) hot / cold 熱 / 冰

(C) Taiwanese Breakfast Drinks

- Soybean Milk 豆漿
- Rice & Peanut Milk 米漿
- Milk Tea 奶茶

Choose the incorrect answer:

1. (   ) Types of traditional Taiwanese breakfast foods:
   (A) pork bun   (B) vegetable bun   (C) small steamed buns   (D) fried turnip bum.
2. (   ) Types of traditional Taiwanese breakfast foods:
   (A) steamed bun (with egg)   (B) sweet potato congee   (C) fried stick   (D) salted soymilk.
3. (   ) Types of traditional Taiwanese breakfast drinks:
   (A) cold soybean milk   (B) oatmilk   (C) rice & peanut milk   (D) hot milk tea.
4. (   ) Types of traditional Taiwanese breakfast foods:
   (A) cheese and onion omelet   (B) sticky rice roll   (C) Taiwanese omelet   (D) turnip cake.
5. (   ) Types of cutlery:
   (A) fork   (B) chopsticks   (C) straw   (D) bean.

REVIEW & IN CLASS PRACTICE

Unit 4

Test Yourself

Mix & match the questions and answers below.

a. thin and crispy	b. mushrooms	c. pepperoni	d. delivery
e. coupons	f. Hawaiian	g. reader	g. toppings

1. A : Texas Pizza! How can I help you?
   B : I'd like to order four _____ pizzas, please.
2. A : Papa John's Pizza. How can I help you?
   B : I'd like to order three medium pizzas, please.
   A : What kind of _____ would you like?
   B : I'd like sausage, _____ and _____, please.
3. A : What kind of crust would you like?
   B : I'd like the _____ crust, please.
4. A : Would that be _____ or pickup?
   B : Pickup, please.
5. A : Do you have any _____ you'd like to use today?
   B : No, I don't.

Match the pictures with the words given below.

Pizza Toppings

a. black olives	b. pepperoni	c. ham	d. red bell pepper
e. green bell pepper	f. shrimp	g. mushrooms	h. calamari

1. _____

2. _____

3. _____

4. _____

5. _____

6. _____

7. _____

8. _____

Choose the right answer

Which of the following is the incorrect answer?

1. (   ) Pizza sizes: (A) slice   (B) Extra Large   (C) jumbo   (D) persona
2. (   ) Types of pizza toppings: (A) crust   (B) green pepper   (C) pineapple   (D) chicken
3. (   ) Types of pizza toppings: (A) sausage   (B) pepperoni   (C) stuffed   (D) cheese
4. (   ) Ways to pick up a pizza: (A) carryout   (B) delivery   (C) pickup   (D) discount
5. (   ) Types of pizza crust: (A) classic   (B) stuffed(cheesy)   (C) jumbo   (D) thin and crispy

Sentence Practice

Rewrite the below sentences in the correct orders.

1. delivery / will / be / pickup / that / or / ?

   _____?

2. one / pepperoni / please / I'd / jumbo / pizza / like / ? / ,

   _____?

3. crust / would / kind / what / of / you / like / ?

   _____?

4. special / today / have / we / a / for

   _____?

5. coupons / you'd / use / today / are / there / any / like / to / ?

   _____?

REVIEW & IN CLASS PRACTICE

Unit 5   Drive-thru' Fast Food Restaurant

Test Yourself

Fill in the blanks with the correct answers:

a. relish	b. drive up	c. Apple Pay	d. Kosher Style
e. barely	f. toppings	g. reader	h. pick up

1. Ken and Michelle are planning to go on a road trip to the countryside. They decided to stop by a drive-thru' at Five Guys Burger & Fries drive-thru' to get a quick lunch.

    Order-taker : Welcome to Five Guys. May I take your order?

    Ken   : I would like to have a _____ hotdog, a cheeseburger, one large fries and a coffee milkshake, please.

    Order-taker : I'm sorry, sir. Can you speak directly into the microphone? I can _____ hear you.

    Ken   : Oh, okay. I would like to have a Kosher Style hotdog, a cheeseburger, one large fries and a coffee milkshake, please.

2. Order-taker : What kind of toppings would you like for your cheeseburger?

    Ken   : How many toppings can I choose?

    Order-taker : You can choose as many as you like.

    Ken   : Oh, okay. I'll have the lettuce, _____ and A1 sauce, please.

3. Order-taker : Would you like anything else?

    Ken   : No, that'll be all.

    Order-taker : Please _____ to the next window.

4. Ken drives up to the next window.

    Server 1   : That'll be $13.27 (thirteen, twenty-seven), please.

    Ken   : Do you accept _____ ?

    Server 1   : Yup! Just a second··· Here's the _____ .

5. Ken holds his cellphone near the reader.

    [Beep!]

    Server 1   : Ok. You're done. Just drive up to the next window to _____your order.

Q & A

Go to the conversation part of this unit. After listening and reading the conversation, answer the following questions:

1. What kind of hotdog did Ken order?

   _____

2. What kind of fries did Ken order?

   _____

3. How many toppings can Ken choose for his little cheeseburger?

   _____

4. What kind of mix-ins did Ken choose for his milkshake?

   _____

5. How did Ken pay for his meal?

   _____

Mix and Match the Chinese-English Translations

a.	配料	1. ( )	road trip
b.	把車子往前開	2. ( )	countryside
c.	蘋果行動支付	3. ( )	drive-thru
d.	配料	4. ( )	order-taker
e.	開車旅行	5. ( )	Kosher Style hotdog
f.	鄉村	6. ( )	speak directly into the microphone
g.	得來速	7. ( )	toppings
h.	訂單接受者	8. ( )	mix-ins
i.	讀卡機	9. ( )	drive up
j.	去領取 (餐點)	10. ( )	Apple Pay
k.	猶太風格熱狗	11. ( )	reader
l.	直接對著麥克風講話	12. ( )	pick up (food)

Choose your own hotdog/burger/sandwich and toppings

Choose your own (A1/A2/A3) hotdog/burger/sandwich with two toppings (B) of your own choice from the menu given below:

Example:

I'd like a <u>Kosher Style hotdog</u> with <u>BBQ sauce</u> and <u>mushrooms</u>, please.
    (A1/A2/A3)   (B)   (B)

1. I'd like a _____ with _____ and _____, please.
    (A1/A2/A3)   (B)   (B)

2. I'd like a _____ with _____ and _____, please.
    (A1/A2/A3)   (B)   (B)

3. I'd like a _____ with _____ and _____, please.
               (A1/A2/A3)   (B)   (B)

4. I'd like a _____ with _____ and _____, please.
               (A1/A2/A3)   (B)   (B)

5. I'd like a _____ with _____ and _____, please.
               (A1/A2/A3)   (B)   (B)

(A1) HOTDOGS 熱狗

- Kosher Style Hotdog 猶太風格熱狗
- Cheese Dog 起司熱狗
- Bacon Dog 培根熱狗
- Bacon Cheese Dog 培根起司熱狗

(A2) BURGERS 漢堡

- Hamburger 漢堡
- Cheeseburger 起司漢堡
- Bacon Burger 培根漢堡
- Bacon Cheeseburger 培根起司漢堡

(A3) SANDWICHES 三明治

- Veggie Sandwich 蔬菜三明治
- Cheese Veggie Sandwich 起司蔬菜三明治
- Grilled Cheese Sandwich 烤起司三明治

BLT 三明治

- 培根、蔬菜、番茄三明治（Bacon, Lettuce, Tomato，簡稱 BLT 三明治）

TOPPINGS 配料

Choose as many as you like! 你可以隨心所欲加選你喜歡的配料！

• A1 Sauce A1 牛排醬	• BBQ Sauce 烤肉醬	• Cheese 起司
• Green Peppers 青椒	• Mushrooms 蘑菇	• Hot sauce 辣醬
• Jalapeno 墨西哥辣椒	• Ketchup 番茄醬	• Lettuce 生菜
• Mayo (mayonnaise) 美乃滋	• Mustard 黃芥末	• Fresh Onions 洋蔥
• Grilled Onions 烤洋蔥	• Pickles 醃黃瓜	• Relish 切碎的酸黃瓜
• Tomatoes 番茄		

Choose your own mix-ins for your milkshake

Choose a milkshake with three choices of mix-ins from the menu given below:

Example:

I'd like a milkshake with <u>Oreo cookies, bacon</u> and <u>banana</u>, please.

1. I'd like a milkshake with _____, _____ and _____, please.
2. I'd like a milkshake with _____, _____ and _____, please.
3. I'd like a milkshake with _____, _____ and _____, please.
4. I'd like a milkshake with _____, _____ and _____, please.
5. I'd like a milkshake with _____, _____ and _____, please.

MILKSHAKE MIX-INS 奶昔配料

Choose as many mix-ins as you like! 你可以隨心所欲加選你喜歡的配料！
- Bacon 培根
- Cherries 櫻桃
- Oreo cookies 奧利奧餅乾
- Bananas 香蕉
- Salted caramel 海鹽焦糖
- Peanut butter 花生醬
- Coffee 咖啡
- Chocolate 巧克力
- Malted Milk 麥芽牛奶
- Strawberries 草莓

Choose the incorrect answer:

1. (   )   Types of burger toppings:

   (A) lettuce   (B) pickles   (C) tomatoes   (D) milkshake.

2. (   )   Types of burger toppings:

   (A) cheese   (B) mushrooms   (C) Kosher   (D) A1 sauce.

3. (   )   Types of burgers:

   (A) ham   (B) cheeseburger   (C) bacon burger   (D) little bacon cheeseburger.

4. (   )   Types of sandwiches:

   (A) veggie sandwich   (B) cheese veggie sandwich   (C) grilled cheese sandwich   (D) Cajun.

5. (   )   Types of milkshake mix-ins:

   (A) cherries   (B) Oreo cookies   (C) bananas   (D) sandwich.

REVIEW & IN CLASS PRACTICE

Unit 6

Test Yourself

Fill in the blanks with the correct answers.

a. venti	b. name	c. to go
d. Americano	e. cream	f. on a diet

1.　A : Hi! How are you doing today? What can I get for you today?

　　B : I'd like to have an _____, please.

2.　A : How would you like your coffee?

　　B : With _____ and two sugar, please.

3.　A : Hi! What can I get for you today?

　　B : Two _____ cappuccino, please.

4.　A : What's your _____?

　　B : It's Christina.

5.　A : For here or _____?

　　B : For here, please.

Match the Chinese-English Translations

1. (　) café	a.	中杯（星巴克專用飲料杯大小名稱）
2. (　) short (coffee size)	b.	咖啡師傅 (門市中調理咖啡的人)
3. (　) tall (coffee size)	c.	大杯（星巴克專用飲料杯大小名稱）
4. (　) grande (coffee size)	d.	特大杯（星巴克專用飲料杯大小名稱）
5. (　) venti (coffee size)	e.	奶精 / 奶球
6. (　) cream / creamer	f.	招呼
7. (　) caramel macchiato	g.	拾起 / 撿起來
8. (　) barista	h.	小杯 (星巴克專用飲料杯大小名稱)
9. (　) hail	i.	焦糖瑪奇朵
10. (　) picked up	j.	咖啡館

Sentence Practice

Rewrite the below sentences in the correct orders.

1. size / would / like / you / what / ?

   _____?

2. four / : / have / we / short / grande / venti/ and / tall / sizes

   _____.

3. coffee / would / you / how / like / your / ?

   _____.

4. please / creams / Two / sugars / and / two / ,

   _____.

Choose the right answer

Which of the following is the incorrect answer?

1. (   ) Starbucks coffee sizes: (A) tall   (B) grand   (C) short   (D) venti.
2. (   ) Coffee sizes: (A) small   (B) large   (C) extra large   (D) taller.
3. (   ) How do you like your coffee?   (A) black   (B) with fresh milk   (B) with lemon   (D) with two sugars.
4. (   ) Coffee drinks: (A) caramel   (B) Americano   (C) latte   (D) cappuccino.
5. (   ) Coffee drinks: (A) espresso   (B) hazelnut   (C) caramel macchiato   (D) vanilla latte.

REVIEW & IN CLASS PRACTICE

Unit 7　Taiwanese Bubble Tea

Test Yourself

Fill in the blanks with the correct answers:

a. regular sugar	b. coconut jelly bubble tea	c. I'll have the same
d. cold, but without ice	e. intake	f. on a diet

1. Cashier　: Welcome to Boba Tea Café. Here's our menu.
   Michelle: There are so many choices! Can you recommend some of your customer's favorites?
   Cashier　: Some of our customer's favorites are the taro bubble milk tea, matcha milk tea, _____ , black Boba milk tea and white Boba milk tea.
   Michelle: I'd like a white Boba milk tea, please.

2. Cashier　: Would you like it hot or cold?
   Michelle: Cold, please.
   Cashier　: How much ice would you like? Regular ice, less ice, half ice, a little ice, and _____ ?
   Michelle: Regular ice, please.

3. Cashier　: How much sugar would you like?
   Michelle: You can even choose how much sugar you want too?!
   Cashier　: Yes! The Taiwanese are very particular about their sugar level _____ .
   There's _____ , less sugar, half sugar, a little sugar and sugar-free.

4. Michelle: _____ . What would you suggest?
   Ken　　: What about half sugar?
   Michelle: Sounds good to me!

5. The cashier then turned to Ken.
   Cashier　: What would you like to have?
   Ken　　: _____ .
   Cashier　: Ok. So, that'll be two large, bubble milk tea? Half sugar, and cold, but without ice.
   Ken　　: That's correct!

Q & A

Go to the conversation part of this unit. After listening and reading the conversation, answer the following questions:

1. What different levels of coldness do they have at the Boba Tea Café?

   _____

2. What does it mean by "cold, but without ice?"

   _____

3. What did Ken order?

   _____

4. How much did Michelle pay the cashier?

   _____

5. How did Michelle and Ken want their bubble teas packaged?

   _____

Mix and Match the Chinese-English Translations

a. 調酒器
b. 茶調理師
c. 排掉水
d. 極冷的 / 冰冷的
e. 火辣辣的夏天太陽
f. 珍珠奶茶店
g. 徒步旅行
h. 糖份水準
i. 引入口 / 納入（數）量
j. 我在減肥

1. (　　) walking tour
2. (　　) scorching summer sun
3. (　　) Boba Tea Café
4. (　　) cocktail mixer
5. (　　) drain
6. (　　) icy-cold
7. (　　) sugar level
8. (　　) intake
9. (　　) I'm on a diet
10. (　　) tea barista

Make your own cup of bubble tea:

Fill in the blanks with the different (A) sizes, (B) hot / cold, (C) sweetness level, and (D) types of tea, with the choices given below:

Example:

I'd like to have a _____medium_____, _____regular ice_____, _____light sugar_____, _____Boba milk tea_____, please.
              (A) size   (B) hot / cold   (C) sweetness level   (D) type of tea

1. I'd like to have a _____, _____, _____, _____, please.
                  (A) size   (B) hot / cold   (C) sweetness level   (D) type of tea

2. I'd like to have a _____, _____, _____, _____, please.
                  (A) size   (B) hot / cold   (C) sweetness level   (D) type of tea

3. I'd like to have a _____, _____, _____, _____, please.
                  (A) size   (B) hot / cold   (C) sweetness level   (D) type of tea

4. I'd like to have a _____, _____, _____, _____, please.
                  (A) size   (B) hot / cold   (C) sweetness level   (D) type of tea

5. I'd like to have a _____, _____, _____, _____, please.
                  (A) size   (B) hot / cold   (C) sweetness level   (D) type of tea

(a) Size 大小

Small 小杯 / Medium 中杯 / Large 大杯 / Extra Large 特大杯

(b) Hot / Cold　熱 / 冷

Regular ice 正常冰	Less ice 少冰	Half ice 半冰	A little ice 微冰	Cold, but without ice 去冰	Room temperature 常溫	Hot 熱的

(c) Sweetness Level 甜度

 100%
Regular Sugar
正常糖

 70%
Less Sugar
七分 / 少糖

 50%
Half Sugar
五分 / 半糖

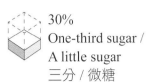 30%
One-third sugar /
A little sugar
三分 / 微糖

 0%
Sugar-free
無糖

(d) Types of tea 茶種類

- Boba milk tea　波霸奶茶
- Black tea macchiato　紅茶瑪奇朵
- Bubble green milk tea　珍珠奶綠
- Bubble milk tea　珍珠奶茶
- Coconut jelly bubble tea　椰果奶茶
- Coffee jelly milk tea　咖啡凍奶茶
- Green bean milk tea　綠豆沙奶茶
- Green milk tea　奶綠
- Green tea latte　綠茶拿鐵
- Hokkaido milk tea with pudding & pearls
  北海道布丁珍奶
- Jasmine milk tea　茉莉奶茶

- Lychee oolong tea　荔枝烏龍茶
- Mango green tea　芒果綠茶
- Matcha latte　抹茶拿鐵
- Matcha milk tea　抹茶奶茶
- Passion fruit green tea　百香綠茶
- Peach black tea　水蜜桃紅茶
- Pudding milk tea　布丁奶茶
- Red bean milk tea　紅豆奶茶
- Roasted milk tea　烤奶茶
- Taro bubble tea　芋頭珍珠奶茶
- Tea latte　奶茶拿鐵
- Winter melon mountain tea　冬瓜清茶

Choose the incorrect answer:

1. (　　) How much ice would you like in your bubble tea?
   (A) less ice　(B) half ice
   (C) ice　(D) cold, but without ice.

2. (　　) How sweet would you like your bubble tea?
   (A) less ice　(B) half sugar
   (C) one ice　(D) sugar-free.

3. (　　) What kind of toppings would you like in your bubble tea?
   (A) green beans　(B) grass
   (C) longan　(D) coconut jelly.

4. (　　) Types of bubble tea:
   (A) coconut　(B) coffee jelly milk tea
   (C) passion fruit green tea　(D) pudding milk tea.

5. (　　) Types of bubble tea:
   (A) green tea latte　(B) Hokkaido
   (C) passion fruit green tea　(D) coffee jelly milk tea.

REVIEW & IN CLASS PRACTICE

Unit 8   Wine

Test Yourself

Fill in the blanks with the correct answers.

a. Chardonnay	b. bottle	c. Malbec
d. Moscato	e. wine opener	f. menu
g. poured		

1. A : Good evening, I'm Kelly. I will be your server tonight.

    B : I'd like to have some red wine tonight.

    A : Sure. Here's our _____.

2. B : What red wine would you recommend?

    A : Two of our customers' favorite red wines are the _____ and _____.

3. C : I prefer white wine.

    A : Some of our customers' favorites are the _____ and _____.

4. A : What can I get for you tonight?

    D : Yes, I'd like a _____ of Sauvignon Blanc, please.

5. The waiter returned with a bottle of Sauvignon Blanc. He opened the bottle with a _____. After the waiter opened the bottle of wine, he _____ some wine into a glass.

Match the Chinese-English Translations

1. (	) nightcap	a.	點頭
2. (	) wine bar	b.	葡萄酒單
3. (	) vintage	c.	開瓶器
4. (	) wine opener	d.	倒
5. (	) cork	e.	輕搖酒杯
6. (	) pour	f.	輕輕的聞
7. (	) swirl	g.	軟木塞
8. (	) whiff	h.	睡前酒
9. (	) nod your head	i.	葡萄酒酒吧
10. (	) wine list / wine menu	j.	葡萄收成年份

Sentence Practice

Rewrite the below sentences in the correct orders.

1. list / Here's / wine / our

    _____.

2. recommend / would / red / you / what / wine / ?

    _____.

3. favorites / Cabernet Sauvignon / are / Some / of / Pinot Noir / and / customers' / our / the / Malbec

   _____.

4. glass / of / I'll / have / a / Chardonnay / please / , /

   _____.

5. I'll / bottle / please / Merlot / of / have / a / , /

   _____.

What would you like? (wine)

Fill in the blanks with different (I) size, (II) country of origin, and (III) type of white/red wine.

Example

I'd like a ___glass___ of _____Spanish_____ _____Airen_____.
     (I)size   (II)country of origin   (III)white/red wine

I.　Size: a glass（一杯）, a bottle（一瓶）
II.　Country of origin: 葡萄酒產地
III. Type of white/red wine: 葡萄酒品種

(II) Country of origin 葡萄酒產地	(III) Types of white/red wines 葡萄酒品種
French　法國	Merlot, Grenache　梅洛、格那希
Spanish　西班牙	Tempranillo, Airén　丹魄、爵愛仁
Argentinian　阿根廷	Malbec, Chardonnay　馬爾貝克、霞多麗
German　德國	Riesling, Müller-Thurgau　麗絲玲、米勒－圖高
Chilean　智利	Cabernet, Chardonnay　卡本內、霞多麗
Italian　義大利	Sangiovese, Trebbiano　山吉歐維榭、特雷比奧羅
American　美國	Cabernet Sauvignon, Chardonnay　卡本內蘇維翁、霞多麗
Australian　澳大利亞	Shiraz, Chardonnay　西拉、霞多麗
South African　南非	Chenin Blanc, Colombard　白梢楠、鴿籠白
Portuguese　葡萄牙	Alvarinho　阿爾瓦裡尼奧

Exercise

1. I'd like a _____ of _____ _____ .
       (I) size (II) country of origin (III) white/ red wine
2. I'd like a _____ of _____ _____ .
       (I) size (II) country of origin (III) white/ red wine
3. I'd like a _____ of _____ _____ .
       (I) size (II) country of origin (III) white/ red wine
4. I'd like a _____ of _____ _____ .
       (I) size (II) country of origin (III) white/ red wine
5. I'd like a _____ of _____ _____ .
       (I) size (II) country of origin (III) white/ red wine

REVIEW & IN CLASS PRACTICE

Unit 9　Taipei Michelin Bib Gourmand Selection

Test Yourself

a. Tonghua	b. take a stroll	c. tender braised pork
d. bowls	e. change	f. Michelin Bib Gourmand
g. Shilin	h. pickled mustard green	

1. Ken and Michelle are discussing which night market to visit tonight.
   Michelle: How should we choose which one to go to?
   Ken　　: May I suggest that we try one that is listed in the Taipei _____?
   Michelle: Great idea!?

2. Michelle: Which night markets are on the Bib Gourmand list?
   Ken　　: Let me see… (Ken started surfing the internet on his smartphone).
   　　　　There's the Raohe night market, _____ night market, Ningxia
   　　　　night market, _____ night market and Gongguan night market.
   Michelle: Let's go to the nearest night market from here.
   Ken　　: Sounds good to me!

3. Ken and Michelle arrived at the Ningxia night market.
   Michelle: Why don't we _____ through the street stalls first, and then see what we'd like to try out?
   Ken　　: Sounds like a great idea!

4. Ken　　: The steamed pork sandwich looks scrumptious. What is it?
   Michelle: It's a fluffy, steamed white bun stuffed with _____, powdered peanuts,_____ and
   　　　　coriander.
   Ken　　: Sounds delicious. I'd like to try that.

5. Ken and Michelle started strolling through the street stalls again.
   Michelle: The sesame oil chicken smells delicious. What's in it?
   Ken　　: It's chicken cooked in sesame oil and ginger broth. It's usually eaten
   during the winter to keep your body warm. Would you like to try it?
   Michelle: Sure. My mouth is watering already!
   Ken　　: Can I have two _____ of sesame oil chicken, please?
   Vendor　: That'll be $380.
   Ken　　: Here's $400.
   Vendor　: $20 is your _____. Please find a table and we'll send your food over.
   {Ken and Michelle found a table and sat down to wait for their food}.

Q & A

Go to the conversation part of this unit. After listening and reading the conversation, answer the following questions:

1. Name five night markets that are on the Bib Gourmand list.

_____

2. Describe the steamed pork sandwich.

_____

3. How much is one steamed pork sandwich?

_____

4. Describe the sesame oil chicken.

_____

5. How much did Ken give the vendor for the sesame oil chicken?

_____

Mix and Match the Chinese-English Translations

a. 米其林指南《必比登夜市小吃》
b. 饒河夜市
c. 通化夜市
d. 寧夏夜市
e. 士林夜市
f. 公館夜市
g. 閒逛 / 漫步 / 慢慢地走
h. 街頭貨攤
i. 美味的
j. 蓬鬆
k. 塞滿…
l. 小販
m. 用 ... 手的
n. 清湯 / 湯
o. 找頭 / 零錢

1. (　　) Gongguan night market
2. (　　) vendor
3. (　　) handed
4. (　　) street stalls
5. (　　) scrumptious
6. (　　) Ningxia night market
7. (　　) Shilin night market
8. (　　) broth
9. (　　) change
10. (　　) Michelin Bib Gourmand
11. (　　) Raohe night market
12. (　　) Tonghua night market
13. (　　) take a stroll
14. (　　) fluffy
15. (　　) stuffed with

Night Market Food ~ Mix and match the Chinese-English Translations

a. 棺材板
b. 擔仔麵
c. 鵝肉
d. 牛肉麵
e. 胡椒餅
f. 滷味
g. 滷肉飯
h. 蚵仔麵線
i. 生煎包
j. 魷魚羹
k. 大腸包小腸
l. 臭豆腐
m. 鹹酥雞
n. 烤魷魚
o. 關東煮
p. 蚵仔煎
q. 碗粿
r. 甜不辣
s. 筒仔米糕

1. (　　) beef noodles
2. (　　) black pepper bun
3. (　　) braised dishes
4. (　　) braised pork rice
5. (　　) coffin bread / deep-fried coffin-shaped sandwich
6. (　　) Danzai noodles (Ta-a noodles)
7. (　　) goose meat
8. (　　) grilled squid
9. (　　) Oden
10. (　　) oyster omelet
11. (　　) oyster vermicelli
12. (　　) pan-fried buns
13. (　　) rice pudding
14. (　　) squid thick soup/squid potage
15. (　　) sticky rice sausage
16. (　　) stinky tofu
17. (　　) Taiwanese-style fried chicken
18. (　　) tempura
19. (　　) tube rice pudding

Choose the incorrect answer:

1. (　　) Names of night markets in Taiwan:
   (A) Linjiang night market　(B) GuanGong night market
   (C) Ningshang night market　(D) Lin night market

2. (　　) Names of night markets in Taiwan:
   (A) Yansan night market　(B) Nanjichang night market
   (C) Xi night Market　(D) Raohe night market

3. (　　) Types of night market foods:
   (A) black pepper bun　(B) stinky　(C) Oden　(D) oyster omelet.

4. (　　) Types of night market foods:
   (A) grilled squid　(B) oyster vermicelli　(C) coffin bread　(D) tube.

5. (　　) Things and people you see in a night market:
   (A) customers　(B) stroll　(C) night market food　(D) street stalls.

REVIEW & IN CLASS PRACTICE

Unit 10   Restaurant Reservations & Corkage Fees

Test Yourself

Fill in the blanks with the correct answers.

a. scoops	b. cup	c. sample
d. toppings	e. cotton candy	

1. Server   : Would you like to try a _____?
    Customer : Can I have a try the mango sorbet, please?
2. Server   : Would you like to try another sample?
    Customer : Can I try the _____, please?
3. Customer : Can I have three _____ of almond ice-cream, please.
4. Server   : Would you like it in a _____ or cone?
    Customer : In a cone, please.
5. Server   : Would you like any _____ on your ice-cream?
    Customer : Yes. Can I have M&M's and Oreo's, please?

Match the Chinese-English Translations

1. ( ) ice-cream parlor	a.	芒果雪酪
2. ( ) sample	b.	甜筒
3. ( ) cotton candy flavor	c.	兩球冰淇淋
4. ( ) tiny plastic spoon	d.	冰淇淋商店
5. ( ) mango sorbet	e.	樣品
6. ( ) cone	f.	加在冰淇淋上面的配料
7. ( ) toppings	g.	一球冰淇淋
8. ( ) one scoop	h.	棉化糖冰淇淋口味
9. ( ) double scoop	i.	極小的塑膠湯匙
10. ( ) triple scoop	j.	三球冰淇淋

Sentence Practice

Rewrite the below sentences in the correct orders.

1. sample / you / try / Would / like / to / a / ?

    _____?

2. taste / not / This / really / is / to / my

    _____.

3. two / please / have / I / Can / scoops / , / ?

    _____?

4. cup / Would / it / in / a / cone / you / like / or / ?

   _____?

5. ice-cream / your / Would / toppings / any / you / like / on / ?

   _____?

Order your own ice-cream

Example:

I'd like to have <u>two</u> scoop(s) of <u>vanilla</u> ice-cream in a <u>cup</u>, please.
             (IA)   (II)   (III)

I'd like to have a <u>single</u> scoop(s) of <u>peppermint</u> ice-cream in a <u>cone</u>, please.
                  (IB)   (II)   (III)

I. How many scoops?

   (IA) one, two, three.

   (IB) single, double, triple.

II. What ice-cream flavor would you like?

• Almond ice-cream 杏仁冰淇淋	• Cappuccino ice-cream 卡布奇諾冰淇淋	• Cheesecake 起司蛋糕冰淇淋
• Hazelnut chocolate ice-cream 榛果巧克力冰淇淋	• Chocolate Chip 巧克力脆片冰淇淋	• Mango sorbet 芒果雪酪冰淇淋
• Chocolate Mint 薄荷巧克力冰淇淋	• Matcha ice-cream 抹茶冰淇淋	• Coconut 椰林冰淇淋
• Mint chocolate ice-cream 薄荷巧克力冰淇淋	• Coffee 咖啡冰淇淋	• Tiramisu ice-cream 提拉米蘇冰淇淋
• Cotton Candy 棉花糖冰淇淋	• Vanilla ice-cream 香草冰淇淋	

III. In a cone or cup?

• Cone

• Cup

1. I'd like to have _____scoop(s) of _____ice-cream in a _____, please.
                  (IA)   (II)   (III)

2. I'd like to have _____scoop(s) of _____ice-cream in a _____, please.
                  (IB)   (II)   (III)

3. I'd like to have _____scoop(s) of _____ice-cream in a _____, please.
                  (IA)   (II)   (III)

4. I'd like to have _____scoop(s) of _____ice-cream in a _____, please.
                  (IB)   (II)   (III)

REVIEW & IN CLASS PRACTICE

Unit 11   Restaurant Reservations & Corkage Fees

Test Yourself

Fill in the blanks with the correct answers.

a. clam chowder	b. medium	c. onion soup	d. mashed potatoes
e. sour cream	f. sirloin steak	g. tomato soup	

1. A : Are you ready to order now?
   B : Yes, we are.
   A : What would you like for your entrée, ma'am?
   B : I'd like a _____, please.
2. A : Ok. How would you like your steak?
   B : _____, please.
3. A : Would you like some soup or salad with that?
   B : What kinds of soup do you have?
   A : We have _____, _____ and _____.
   B : I'll have an onion soup, please.
4. A : Would you like a baked potato or _____?
   B : Baked potato, please.
   A : Would you like _____ on that?

Match the Chinese-English Translations

1. ( ) Steakhouse	a.	蛤蜊巧達濃湯
2. ( ) Filet Mignon	b.	牛排館
3. ( ) Ribeye steak	c.	菲力牛排
4. ( ) T-bone steak	d.	肋眼牛排
5. ( ) New York Strip	e.	沙朗牛排
6. ( ) Sirloin steak	f.	紐約客牛排
7. ( ) Clam chowder	g.	主菜
8. ( ) Entrée	h.	烤馬鈴薯
9. ( ) Baked potato	i.	丁骨牛排
10. ( ) Mashed potatoes	j.	洋蔥湯
11. ( ) Sour cream	k.	馬鈴薯泥
12. ( ) Onion soup	l.	酸奶

Sentence Practice

Rewrite the below sentences in the correct orders.

1. entrée / your / like / would / you / what / for / ?

   _____?

2. steak / how / like / your / would / you / ?

   _____?

3. baked / like / a / would / you / mashed / potato / potatoes / or / ?

   _____?

4. soup / or / would / you / like / salad / ?

   _____?

Choose the right answer

Which is the incorrect answer?

1. (   ) Types of steaks: (A) Yorker   (B) filet mignon   (C) sirloin   (D) short ribs
2. (   ) Types of steaks: (A) filet   (B) ribeye   (C) New York Strip   (D) porterhouse
3. (   ) How would you like your steak?   (A) rare   (B) regular   (C) medium   (D) well-done
4. (   ) How would you like your steak?   (A) medium-rare   (B) medium-well   (C) well   (D) medium
5. (   ) Types of sides: (A) mashed potatoes   (B) tomato soup   (B) baked potato   (D) sour cream.

REVIEW & IN CLASS PRACTICE

Unit 12   Donuts

Test Yourself

a. original glazed	b. tap-to-pay	c. folks	d. debit
e. lining up	f. pick up	g.having over	

1. It's Christmas Eve. Michelle and Ken are planning to have some friends over for a Christmas party the next day. They are _____ at the Donut Hole to _____some donuts for their Christmas party tomorrow.

2. Ken   : Honey, how many donuts do you think we should get for our party tomorrow?

   Michelle: Let's see... How many guests are we _____?

   Ken   : There's Christina, Justin, Janet, Sam, Britney... Hmmm... About 20 people.

   Michelle: What about two to three dozen donuts?

   Ken   : Sounds good to me!

3. Ken started looking at the menu on the wall.

   Ken   : Honey, they have _____ donuts and assorted variety donuts.

   Michelle: I'd like to get at least a box of festive donuts.

   Ken   : I agree!

4. It was Ken and Michelle's turn.

   Server   : Next! Merry Christmas, _____! Can I help you?

   Ken   : Merry Christmas to you too! We'd like to have half a dozen original glazed donuts, one dozen assorted variety donuts and one dozen festive donuts, please.

   Server   : Sure.

5. The server then passed the donuts to the cashier...

   Cashier : That'll be $5.99 (five, ninety-nine) for half a dozen glazed donuts, $9.99 (nine, ninety-nine) for a dozen assorted variety donuts and $10.99 (ten, ninety-nine) for a dozen festive donuts. Your total comes up to $26.97 (twenty-six, ninety-seven). Will that be _____or credit?

   Ken   : Debit, please.

   Cashier : Just place your card on the reader and _____..

Q & A

Go to the conversation part of this unit. After listening and reading the conversation, answer the following questions:

1. Where did Michelle and Ken pick up donuts for their Christmas party?
_____

2. How many guests were Ken and Michelle expecting for their Christmas party?
_____

3. What donuts did Michelle and Ken think would certainly "pump up the Christmas spirit"?
_____

4. How many donuts is one dozen?
_____

5. How many and what type of donuts did Michelle pick for their assorted varieties?
_____

6. How did Ken pay for the donuts?
_____

Match the Chinese-English Translations

a. 一打（12入）
b. 經典糖霜甜甜圈
c. 節日氣氛
d. 至少
e. 聖誕老人肚皮
f. 簽帳金融卡
g. 半打（6入）
h. 人們〔古、方〕
i. 我打賭 / 我敢斷定 / 我確信
j. 提升耶誕氣氛
k. 排隊
l. 零接觸支付服務
m. 買東西
n. 綜合口味甜甜圈
o. 感應讀卡機

1. (　　) lining up
2. (　　) pickup
3. (　　) assorted variety donuts
4. (　　) reader
5. (　　) at least
6. (　　) Santa's Belly
7. (　　) debit card
8. (　　) Tap-to-pay
9. (　　) half a dozen
10. (　　) one dozen
11. (　　) original glazed donuts
12. (　　) festive mood
13. (　　) I bet
14. (　　) Pump up the Christmas spirit
15. (　　) folks

Number, Prices & Calculations

Based on the below menu, count the total number of donuts and total price of the donuts based on the following #Customer Orders 1,2 and 3, and then write down your answers in the given boxes.

TYPE OF DONUT	HALF DOZEN	DOZEN	ONE / SINGLE
ORIGINAL GLAZED DONUTS	$5.99	$8.99	$0.99
ASSORTED VARIETY DONUTS	$6.99	$9.99	$1.09
FESTIVE VARIETY DONUTS	$7.99	$10.99	$1.29

Example:

I'd like to have half a dozen original glazed donuts, one dozen assorted variety donuts and half a dozen festive donuts, please.

Type of donut	Number of donuts	Price for each type of donut
Original glazed donuts	6	$5.99
Assorted variety donuts	12	$9.99
Festive donuts	6	$7.99
Total number of donuts	24 donuts	
Total price of donuts		$23.97

1. # Customer Order 1

I'd like to have half a dozen original glazed donuts, two assorted variety donuts and one dozen festive donuts, please.

Type of donut	Number of donuts	Price for each type of donut
Original glazed donuts		$
Assorted variety donuts		$
Festive donuts		$
Total number of donuts	donuts	-
Total price of donuts		$

2. # Customer Order 2

I'd like to have five original glazed donuts, one dozen assorted variety donuts and eight festive donuts, please.

Type of donut	Number of donuts	Price for each type of donut
Original glazed donuts		$
Assorted variety donuts		$
Festive donuts		$
Total number of donuts	donuts	-
Total price of donuts		$

3. # Customer Order 3

I'd like to have two dozen original glazed donuts and three dozen festive donuts, please.

Type of donut	Number of donuts	Price for each type of donut
Original glazed donuts		$
Assorted variety donuts		$
Festive donuts		$
Total number of donuts	donuts	-
Total price of donuts		$

Choose the incorrect answer

1. (   ) Types of donuts:

      (A) original glazed donuts   (B) assorted variety donuts

      (C) festive donuts   (D) debit card donuts

2. (   ) Types of donuts:

      (A) reader donuts   (B) chocolate iced with sprinkles donuts

      (C) salted caramel donuts   (D) almond white chocolate donuts

3. (   ) Types of festive donuts:

      (A) Tree of Hope Donuts   (B) Santa Belly Donuts

      (C) Rudolph Donuts   (D) Pump up the Christmas spirit

4. (   ) Number of donuts (counting donuts):

      (A) single   (B) half dozen   (C) one dozen   (D) two dozen.

5. (   ) Ways to pay for your donuts:

      (A) debit card   (B) credit card   (C) tap-and-go   (D) contact.

✂ （請由此線剪下）

歡迎加入 全華會員

● 會員獨享

會員享購書折扣、紅利積點、生日禮金、不定期優惠活動…等。

● 如何加入會員

掃 QRcode 或填妥讀者回函卡直接傳真 (02) 2262-0900 或寄回，將由專人協助登入會員資料，待收到 E-MAIL 通知後即可成為會員。

如何購買 全華書籍

1. 網路購書

全華網路書店「http://www.opentech.com.tw」，加入會員購書更便利，並享有紅利積點回饋等各式優惠。

2. 實體門市

歡迎至全華門市（新北市土城區忠義路 21 號）或各大書局選購。

3. 來電訂購

(1) 訂購專線：(02) 2262-5666 轉 321-324
(2) 傳真專線：(02) 6637-3696
(3) 郵局劃撥（帳號：0100836-1 戶名：全華圖書股份有限公司）

※ 購書未滿 990 元者，酌收運費 80 元。

OpenTech 全華網路書店 .com.tw

全華網路書店 www.opentech.com.tw
E-mail: service@chwa.com.tw

※ 本會員制如有變更則以最新修訂制度為準，造成不便請見諒。

讀者回函卡

掃 QRcode 線上填寫 ▶▶

姓名：_____　生日：西元_____年____月____日　性別：□男 □女

電話：（　　）_____　手機：_____

e-mail：（必填）_____

通訊處：□□□□□

學歷：□高中・職 □專科 □大學 □碩士 □博士

職業：□工程師 □教師 □學生 □軍・公 □其他

學校／公司：_____　科系／部門：_____

註：數字零，請用 Φ 表示，數字 1 與英文 L 請另註明並書寫端正，謝謝。

・需求書類：
　□A. 電子 □B. 電機 □C. 資訊 □D. 機械 □E. 汽車 □F. 工管 □G. 土木 □H. 化工 □I. 設計
　□J. 商管 □K. 日文 □L. 美容 □M. 休閒 □N. 餐飲 □O. 其他

・本次購買圖書為：_____　書號：_____

・您對本書的評價：
　封面設計：□非常滿意 □滿意 □尚可 □需改善，請說明_____
　內容表達：□非常滿意 □滿意 □尚可 □需改善，請說明_____
　版面編排：□非常滿意 □滿意 □尚可 □需改善，請說明_____
　印刷品質：□非常滿意 □滿意 □尚可 □需改善，請說明_____
　書籍定價：□非常滿意 □滿意 □尚可 □需改善，請說明_____
　整體評價：請說明_____

・您在何處購買本書？
　□書局 □網路書店 □書展 □團購 □其他

・您購買本書的原因？（可複選）
　□個人需要 □公司採購 □親友推薦 □老師指定用書 □其他

・您希望全華以何種方式提供出版訊息及特惠活動？
　□電子報 □DM □廣告 （媒體名稱_____）

・您是否上過全華網路書店？（www.opentech.com.tw）
　□是 □否　您的建議_____

・您希望全華出版哪方面書籍？_____

・您希望全華加強哪些服務？_____

感謝您提供寶貴意見，全華將秉持服務的熱忱，出版更多好書，以饗讀者。

填寫日期：___/___/___

2020.09 修訂

親愛的讀者：

　　感謝您對全華圖書的支持與愛護，雖然我們很慎重的處理每一本書，但恐仍有疏漏之處，若您發現本書有任何錯誤，請填寫於勘誤表內寄回，我們將於再版時修正，您的批評與指教是我們進步的原動力，謝謝！

全華圖書 敬上

勘 誤 表

書號	頁數	行數	書名	作者
			錯誤或不當之詞句	建議修改之詞句

我有話要說：（其它之批評與建議，如封面、編排、內容、印刷品質等……）